FROM FAKING TO FOREVER

STARLING BAY BOOK 4

SIENNA CARR

Author's Note

~

From Faking to Forever is a STANDALONE romance. It is the 4th book in the ***Starling Bay*** series. While you do not need to have read the first three books, it might enhance your reading experience if you do, because many of the characters in this book appear in the other Starling Bay books.

Starling Bay Series:

Whirlwind Kisses
Winter's Kiss
Maid for Him
Love Letters
Escape to Starling Bay (Books 1-3)
From Faking to Forever
Winter's Vow
Guarded Hearts
Table for Two
A Bouquet of Charm
Christmas Hope

Newsletter sign up: http://www.siennacarr.com/newsletter

CHAPTER 1

*E*ight legs. Shay couldn't stop looking at the spider's long, spindly legs, and the mean way he was looking at her. She jumped back. Was it really possible that something so small could cause her so much fear? She didn't like his beady little eyes.

Her heart thumped wildly, because the danger was real.

She reached for her insect catcher, which was always conveniently placed nearby. With the long-handled contraption in her hand, she crawled along the floor, shivering with horror as she tried to trap it in the little compartment. This was the tricky part. The spider crawled away, and she tried again until she finally managed to trap it. She flinched as she stared at it, even trapped, it still felt to her as if it was crawling along her bare skin. "Eww," she winced, rising slowly from the floor, then pointed the bug-catcher out of the window, and released the unwanted intruder.

At times like this she missed having Jenna around. Jenna had no fear of these things. Maybe she was better prepared for them because of her cleaning jobs.

Not that Jenna would ever resort to any more cleaning jobs.

Not now that she was happily dating Reed Knight, one of Starling Bay's wealthiest men.

It reminded her that she still needed to catch up with Jenna because her friend wanted to tell her all about her visit to Montana, a few weeks ago when she went along with Reed to the ranch where his parents lived.

They had been trying to meet up but with both of them busy at work, and Jenna obviously spending a lot of her spare time with Reed, setting a date had so far proved impossible. Plus, with Shay's father recovering from his recent lung cancer surgery, she'd had no free time to herself, and spent the weekends at her parents' place.

At least she'd get to see Jenna tonight with the monthly business owner's social at the town hall. Jenna now worked for Hyacinth Fitzsimmons, Starling Bay's self-proclaimed busybody, and she was responsible for the admin side of tonight's meeting, namely the attendee list and the refreshment table.

These monthly meetings enabled all the business owners to mingle and network. Everyone was welcome, but it was mainly comprised of professional people, most of whom owned their own businesses. Shay and Francine attended every month because it was an opportunity to network and bring in more business for the recruitment company which Francine owned, and for which Shay worked.

She set the bug-catcher down, then brushed the dust off her skirt then noticed she had a stain on it.

Darn it.

She was already running late and Francine was a stickler for her Monday morning meetings. Rushing into her bedroom, Shay pulled out another skirt from her closet, then shimmied out of the one she was wearing when the phone went off. She answered quickly, pulling the new skirt on. "Hello," she said, doing up the zipper as she balanced the phone on her shoulder and tilted her head.

"Is this Miss Donovan?"

It was a voice she didn't recognize. "Yes." She tugged at her blouse from under her skirt so that her blouse was smooth.

"Miss Shay Donovan?"

"Yes." Irritation crept into her voice. "Who is this?"

"I'm calling from Dubois, Barclay and Kleinmeister."

Who? This was different to the usual prank calls she received. She rolled her eyes because this was sucking up time she didn't have, and she was already late for work. "Sorry, I'm not interested in whatever you have to sell." And she hung up.

When the phone rang a second time, she cut it off, then grabbed her handbag and her cell phone, cast her eye over the apartment one more time, her eyes lasering in on the lookout for more creepy crawlies. Finding nothing, she breathed a sigh of relief then closed the door behind her.

CHAPTER 2

Great. Another pregnancy.

Blake, held his head in his hands as Ellen, the latest member from his office administration team, left his office having announced the third pregnancy in the team of four ladies.

This was the last thing he needed first thing on a Monday morning. He had no doubt that Ellen was now happily going around the office and factory floor spreading her happy news, which would take up an hour out of her work this morning.

"What's wrong?" Ralph asked walking in. His general foreman wandered in from time to time. He was in charge of all the operations on the factory floor and reported to Blake. He often offered more than general feedback regarding the day-to-day production details. Ralph also seemed to know everything that went on, and part of the reason was because his wife Nancy headed up the administration office.

At least Nancy wouldn't be surprising him with pregnancy news. She and Ralph had become grandparents for the first time.

"Ellen's pregnant."

"You didn't have anything to do with that did you?" Ralph asked him, chortling at his own silly joke.

"Do you really think?" Blake didn't intend to finish the sentence. For a fifty-something, happily married man, and a recent grandfather, Ralph was supposed to be the voice of reason. Sometimes Blake looked to him to bounce ideas off, but sometimes, like now, the guy could come out with some silly things.

"I blame the office chair," Ralph chortled. "You need to get it replaced. I swear each time one of those women sit on it, they get pregnant."

"You'd better hope that Nancy doesn't sit on it," he threw back, folding his arms with satisfaction at the worried look on Ralph's face.

"We've just become grandparents for the first time. I assure you, Nancy won't be announcing any such news now, or ever. But you…" Ralph pointed a finger at him. "Isn't it about high time you got your head out of your computer and met some nice young woman? It's been a while since you did any of that."

"Women?" Blake snorted. No thank you. Callie French had been the last woman he'd dated, but that had been over a year ago. He'd been pleased when it had ended. They both had.

"You can dismiss it all you want now, but you're going to end up old and lonely if you don't do something about it soon."

"I'm not interested in doing anything about it soon," he growled, needing to get on with his work.

"And who are you going to pass on this company to?"

"Just because you've had a grandchild, doesn't mean you have to lecture to me about offspring."

"I could always hook you up with my niece. She's around your age and gorgeous. I'd rather her meet a decent guy than try any of these dating websites."

Not the niece again. Blake sucked in his breath. "Thanks for the compliment, but no."

Ralph planted his hands on his hips, and looked down at him. "Let me guess, you've been here all day and probably most of the night too."

Blake didn't reply at first. He did spend a lot of time here, but he also went home to get changed and showered. Still, he was doing twelve to fourteen hour days, easily. This business took up his life. It wasn't easy running a factory which manufactured rubber flooring tiles as well as luxury vinyl tile for residential and commercial use. It was a small floundering company when he'd bought it a few years ago, but he'd managed to get it back on track and make it profitable. Ralph and Nancy and most of the employees had stayed on when he took over, but he had expanded considerably in a few short years, to the point that the expansion was leaving a hole in his profits, and the business was taking up all of his time. He didn't have the time or the energy to think about women.

"And what if I did?" he asked, finally.

"Did you do anything this weekend? Go out, meet any people, circulate, have a social life? The chances of you meeting a woman are less than my chances of losing any weight." He patted his potbelly with pride.

Blake stared up testily. "So what if I was here all weekend?" He was the one whose neck was on the line. He was responsible for the wages of his employees, not Ralph. Not anyone else. He sat back, placed his hands on the back of his neck, and pondered his latest problem. "Three pregnancies," he muttered. "Why now? Why all at the same time?"

Ralph chuckled. "It happens, especially if you're happily married."

While he was happy for those who were happily married and

pregnant, this didn't bode well for his business; even though business was booming and sales were increasing every single year.

It was a great position to be in, but it would put a dent in his business because he needed everything to continue to flow. He needed three able replacements for the women who would go on maternity leave.

On top of that, he'd recently had some renovations done, a new outbuilding for storage, and had plans to expand the factory floor some more. He was trying to rein in his expansion, as he knew this could cause potential problems further down the line and he didn't want to grow too fast, then fizzle out and die. Slow and steady was his plan, but random things out of the blue continued to give him financial and logistical headaches.

"I need three replacements in the next six months." Dionne and Penny had announced their pregnancies a few weeks ago, and Ellen just now. That was three quarters of his admin team gone. Poof!

"You can talk to those fine ladies from the recruitment agency," Ralph suggested, with a wink. "Seeing that you've got that meeting tonight."

True. He was attending the monthly meeting at the town hall. Lately, these were his only social outlet, and he found himself looking forward to them.

He would speak to Francine and Shay. They were nice and he'd had plenty of business dealings with them in the past. They were the answer to his short-term employee problems.

Things were suddenly looking a little brighter.

He wasn't averse to seeing Shay Donovan. She was practical, and down to earth, and quite easy on the eye. He found her endearing, and funny. There was nothing romantic between them, but a love-hate dialog often ensued when he spoke to her. He found her endearing, always pushing up her spectacles, and coming out with some funny comments, and this was as much as he could handle right now.

No romance, just a pleasant and friendly encounter. Nothing more.

CHAPTER 3

"We should meet up," Jenna said.

"So you keep saying. You're the one who's always too busy to meet." She couldn't help but admire Jenna's new hair style. No more blue tipped ends, she had cut those off months ago, when the whole thing about her and Reed came out, and Reed's split with his then fiancée happened, but she now had it styled differently. It was shoulder length but with a fringe that framed her face, and she looked more polished. Was that the right word? Certainly, Jenna looked better than ever.

Shay ran a hand over her own hair, then smoothed out an imaginary crease in her skirt. She had never felt self-conscious before, but she did now. It wasn't even that she was jealous of her friend; Jenna deserved every happiness, and she was happy that her friend had finally found it with Reed Knight, but it highlighted the lack of these things in her own life in a way that she had never noticed before.

Jenna had hit the big leagues in one fell swoop. Who would have thought that Shay getting her friend a job as a maid would lead to romance? She was happy for her friend, she really was, but why did she suddenly feel as if she had been left behind?

"You're busy too," Jenna replied.

"How about tomorrow?" Shay suggested. She could do with a girlie chat. Ever since Jenna had moved out of her apartment a few months ago she had missed her company. Jenna moving in had only been a temporary fix because when she had first returned to Starling Bay, she was so broke that she couldn't afford to rent a place of her own. Shay had offered to let her friend stay with her for as long as she needed.

It wasn't only that Jenna was good at getting rid of spiders and other creepy-crawlies, but it was nice not to go home to an empty apartment.

"Tomorrow is good! And you can see my new place!"

"I'd forgotten about that."

"It's lovely," Jenna replied, but she was looking at Reed who was standing almost halfway across the room, talking to someone.

"Can't you at least look at me while you're here?" Shay tapped her friend gently on the shoulder. This had to be love. They'd only just got back after spending a week in Montana and she still couldn't keep her eyes off Reed Knight.

Shay looked over, because wherever Reed was, his friend Rourke was sure to be close by. Rourke was handsome and charming, and she had always enjoyed his company. She had found him some new employees recently, and had also met him a few times through Jenna. Sadly, according to the latest update from her friend, Rourke was no longer a single man.

Shay would never have made a move on the guy; she was not that way inclined, but she would have happily admired him from a distance as long as he was single, which wasn't often, according to the stories she'd heard.

At heart, she was still an old-fashioned gal, preferring the man to do the asking out, but in the past the town hall meetings definitely had an allure to them because she knew there was always a chance to see Rourke.

And *seeing* was about as far as Shay was ever prepared for things to go.

"Come with me," Jenna hissed, causing Shay to turn her head and walk quickly, following Jenna. "I need to do a last minute check on the refreshments."

"How's that working out, having Hyacinth as a boss?"

Jenna eyed the bottles of sparkling and still water, and the bowls of fruit and donuts. "We need more donuts," she answered, before looking up. "Hyacinth?" She laughed. She's a friendly dragon, she's harmless, if you stay in her good graces, and know how to handle her."

"And I'm sure you do."

"I've dealt with Pennington, remember."

Pennington was Reed's manservant whom Jenna had found difficult to get on with. But she seemed to have a knack for turning dragons into friends.

If Reed's ex-fiancée was anything to go by, and if Jenna had been more like her, then dating one of Starling Bay's wealthiest men would have meant she no longer had to work, but Jenna wasn't like that. She, like Shay, was fiercely independent and liked to earn her way. Also, being under Hyacinth's wing had helped Jenna shed some of the stigma she'd had to deal with as a result of the false rumors that Reed's ex had spread. The townspeople had wrongly believed that Jenna had been responsible for Reed and his fiancée splitting up.

"I'll be back," she said, turning to go, presumably to find more donuts.

Left alone, Shay looked around the room to see if Francine had arrived, but she couldn't find her. The meeting would start soon, and she was hungry. She stared at the few donuts left in the basket, then played mental ping-pong as she decided on what to have. She weighed up the pros and cons, and finally picked up a banana to eat quickly now.

Maybe she'd have a donut as a treat later.

CHAPTER 4

"Ijust got back from Montana," Reed told him. "Went to see my parents at the ranch, and I wanted them to meet Jenna properly." Reed singled out his girlfriend who was over by the refreshment table, talking to Shay Donovan.

The sight of Shay made him smile. He had wondered if she would be here tonight, as she usually was, but he hadn't seen her or Francine earlier. He'd go over to Shay later once he'd caught up with Reed. The two of them had had a lot of business dealings in the past, and had met through one of these town hall meetings years ago.

It turned out that Reed Knight was the man to know. He had lots of contacts not only in the small town, but also business contacts far and wide.

"How was Montana?" he asked, eager to know. Reed had hinted at a couple of things in the past, namely his public breakup with his fiancée, and the news spreading like wildfire about him taking up with the maid. That was the problem with living in a small town sometimes. Gossip spread at the speed of light.

"It was awkward at first, but great towards the end. Jenna and my parents got on really well. Being out in the countryside, with the wide open sky and fresh air did us both some good."

"You sound as if you needed to get away," suggested Blake.

"Business takes up too much of our lives. I didn't realize how much until we went away. I mean, I've been able to get away a lot, but it's been business travel mainly. This was different, taking time out and relaxing." He nudged Blake gently, "You know how it is, we somehow get swallowed up with the work, no time to play."

"I hear you." Ralph's words came back at him.

"It's even better when you get away with the right person," said Reed, staring at his girlfriend again.

"Good for you." Blake was happy for the guy.

"At least the old movie theater project is over." Reed's features relaxed and he sighed.

"I walked past it the other day. It looks awesome. You did a great job." He'd gone over to Fellini's for a business meeting, and had seen the old movie theater which was close by. Reed's people had done a spectacular job.

"Wait until you see what it looks like inside."

It hadn't even occurred to him to think about the inside, but knowing Reed, he wouldn't be surprised. This man didn't cut corners. In that respect they were alike. Blake also wanted the best for his business, and had recently upgraded all the machinery and tools, and provided up-to-date training for his employees. The expenses were adding up and biting him right now, but he felt confident he'd made the right decisions for the long-term.

"You'll have to come to the opening night," Reed told him. "It's in the middle of next month. I'll put you on the guest list. You and a plus one?"

Blake laughed that off. "Nope, just me."

"No plus one?" Reed looked surprised. Not that they talked about their love lives much. He and Reed weren't that good of friends to discuss those matters. Their conversations were usually limited to business matters, but Reed telling him about Jenna meeting his parents seemed to have obviously shifted things for him enough that he now seemed at ease asking Blake about his love life.

"No time for it."

"These things fall into place and happen at their own pace," Reed said, before shaking his head. "Sorry. I didn't mean to sound like one of the people who suddenly start preaching, especially about relationships. I'm not that kind of guy."

"I was beginning to think you'd met the right woman and changed."

Reed laughed. "I'm still the same me, and Jenna's still the same Jenna. Being together though, that's a third entity altogether."

"I'll take your word for it. I have other troubles to deal with," Blake replied. "Maternity leave headaches to deal with."

Reed's eyes opened wide, then narrowed. "Did I miss something? I didn't even know you were with someone."

"Not me," he retorted. "My admin team. Three out of the four are pregnant, and they're all leaving around Christmas time. I need to find replacements."

"All at the same time?" Reed replied, grinning. "Must be something in the water."

"Ralph my foreman thinks it's something do with one of the chairs in the office." He shook his head at that. Reed chuckled.

"You should speak to Francine, from the recruitment agency. She's usually good."

"I know. I've dealt with that agency before. Francine's great, but I haven't seen her here tonight."

Blake glanced over at Shay and saw that she was still talking to Jenna. He should go and speak to her about his employee problem now because he needed to rush off at the end. He had a few months yet to sort things out but it would give him a good excuse to talk to Shay if he brought the topic up now. "I might have a word with Shay," he said, seeing Jenna wander off and leave Shay by herself. Now was his chance to grab her. "Let me go and speak to her now. I'll see you around."

"I need to go and hide," Reed muttered. "Hyacinth's found me."

"Didn't realize you were hiding." They shook hands, and he strode over to the refreshment table where Shay had her back to him.

He tapped her on the shoulder and she turned around with her mouth full and a banana in her hand. She coughed, then seemed to splutter, then her face turned red.

At first he didn't know what to make of it, but as she coughed and spluttered some more, he quickly saw that she was actually choking right in front of his eyes. Without waiting another second, he stood behind her, made a fist with one hand, grabbed it with his other hand, and pushed hard a few times under her ribcage.

Something shot from her mouth and rocketed towards the wall. Shay stumbled backwards, wiping her mouth, her face and eyes red. Jenna had come running.

"What happened?" she asked, but he quickly grabbed some napkins from the table and handed them to Shay. A few other people surrounded them and a crowd has formed around Shay. She held her hand to her chest, and looked as if she wanted to die —from embarrassment. "Are you okay?" he asked, still concerned.

She nodded, unable to speak.

Jenna started fussing over her friend, so he left her to it and started to make the crowd disperse. "Nothing to see," he said, smiling good-naturedly and standing in front of Shay so that they couldn't see her.

He was glad he'd been around.

Or maybe he'd been the reason she'd choked, him surprising her so suddenly?

"I have to go," said Jenna, suddenly looking around the room as everyone went to their chair. "Do you mind keeping an eye on her?"

"Not at all." He stepped forward while Jenna picked up Shay's half-eaten banana from the floor.

"Are you okay?" he asked Shay, facing her directly this time.

She nodded and reached for the glass of water he'd poured for her.

"Thank you."

"Don't mention it."

"And thank you for getting rid of the audience."

"Don't mention it," he insisted, then peered at her because her face was red, and she still didn't look well.

"I can't breathe. I think I need some fresh air."

"Come on outside," he offered, and gently took her arm to help her out. Not that she was incapable of walking, but he felt genuinely concerned for her. He could miss Hyacinth's opening note. He usually yawned his way through that part. Networking and meeting other people were what these meetings were best for. And saving Shay Donovan from choking on a banana had already been the highlight of his evening.

CHAPTER 5

What in the world had just happened? It was bad enough she had choked, and worse that it had been on a banana, and even worse that Blake Kennedy, the rough and rugged owner of Kennedy Tiles had performed the Heimlich maneuver on her.

She wanted to hide under the refreshment table and stay there.

"Thanks," she said, feeling better now that they were outside.

"Not a problem, please stop thanking me. Of course, I won't stop reminding you that I saved your life."

"I'm sure you won't. I wouldn't be surprised to see it mentioned in the Starling Bay Daily," she shot back, with some of the usual snarkiness that was a hallmark of their exchanges.

"That's an excellent idea. Thanks for the suggestion. If only I'd taken a picture when you were actually choking."

"Oh no," she replied, exaggerating her look of horror. "I can re-enact the scene for you if you'd like."

"But then I'd have to give you the Heimlich maneuver all over again."

She shivered, with exaggeration and then wiped her mouth with the napkins he'd given her. In all the time she'd known him, she'd never seen this caring and concerned side to him. It was eye-opening, and she was grateful. "You can go back inside," she told him. "I'll be fine out here."

"And leave you here all alone?" He scratched his chin, forcing her attention to the tiny dark hairs that were sprinkled over the lower half of his face. Something about the abrupt and embarrassing Heimlich move made her feel a little shy in front of him, all of a sudden. It was a feeling she wasn't used to, not with Blake Kennedy.

"I'll stay with you a few seconds," he said. "Can't have you passing out. You're still as red as an ruby red tomato."

She winced. "Don't ever take to writing poetry."

"I won't." He smiled at her. "Can I get you something? Another banana perhaps, seeing that you didn't get a chance to finish the last one?"

She narrowed her eyes at him. "You could get me a banana, and I could use it to plug that hole that you use for a mouth."

"Ouch." Now he winced with mock exaggeration, but she found herself staring into his cool gray eyes for a second longer than she should have. Choking on that thing had made her feel all funny.

Fresh air was all she needed.

Not Blake Kennedy reminding her that he had saved her life. If he hadn't tapped her shoulder and taken her by surprise, she might not have choked. Her stomach pitter-pattered as she thought about his hands under her chest, and his body so close behind her.

"You're missing the meeting," she said, eager for him to leave. "I'll be fine out here, really. You should go." For some reason, she felt odd talking to him out here, with it being just the two of them.

"If I didn't know you that well, I'd think you wanted to get rid of me."

She gave him an apologetic smile and tried to cover it. "I'm fine now. I'm still alive, and I'll be eternally indebted to you for rescuing me from a rogue banana."

He laughed. "Glad to be of service."

When her cell phone rang, she pounced on it as if it was her exit strategy.

"Is this Shay Donovan?"

She frowned. The voice at the other end sounded familiar. "Yes. And you are?"

"It's Frank Barclay from the law firm Dubois, Barclay and Kleinmeister."

Francine rushed past her, giving her a wink before she disappeared inside the town hall.

"Who?" Shay asked, momentarily distracted.

"Frank Barclay. I called you this morning."

She blinked, realizing why it was so familiar. This was the same hoax call from earlier one, except now that she wasn't scared about rogue spiders, or focused on zipping up her skirt.

Now that she was able to pay proper attention to the person speaking, it didn't sound like a hoax call at all.

"Law firm?" she asked weakly. Had somebody sued her? Did she have some unpaid parking tickets? Her nerves prickled. This was as bad as a call from the police station.

Blake thumbed to indicate that he was going inside, and mouthed the same as well. She nodded.

"Yes, Ma'am."

"What do you want?"

"I have some good news for you," the man replied. "You are the great niece of Dena Jeffreys aren't you?"

"Who?"

"Dena Jeffreys, from Savannah, Georgia."

Her brow wrinkled as she tried to remember. The name rang a bell, and she remembered that there was a branch of the family, on her mother's side that she had heard about, but they didn't keep in touch. Dena Jeffreys. It was a hard name to forget. "Why?" she asked, suspiciously.

"I'm sorry to inform you that your Great Aunt passed away two weeks ago. She was a hundred and three."

Shay blinked. She felt a sense of shame that she didn't know this woman, and felt that this news should make her feel sad, but she didn't know her. They had never met. At least, she was sure they hadn't met.

"We need to speak in person, Miss Donovan. There is the delicate matter of your Great Aunt's will. She has named you as the sole beneficiary."

"She's what?" *Will? Sole beneficiary?* No, it couldn't be.

"The *recipient*, Miss Donovan." The lawyer's clipped tone did nothing to clear the fog and she shook her head in disbelief. "There's been a mistake." She pinched herself, because the events of this evening were taking on a most surreal tone. "I...I don't think you... I don't think you have the right person. What if there's another Shay Donovan?"

"You are familiar with Dena Jeffreys who married a British soldier in England?"

She tilted her head. Yes. It sounded like it was the same person. But this couldn't be real. It had to be a joke.

"In any case, Miss Donovan, Mrs. Jeffreys' estate has exact written instructions. This is why it was easy for us to find you. Would it be okay for me to fly over to meet with you? There are stipulations to the will because of the sum involved, and we are running out of time."

She stumbled back a few steps. "What do you mean we're running out of time?" And then she gasped. "The sum involved? How much are we talking?"

"I'm not at liberty to disclose anything further over the phone, Miss Donovan. I'm afraid it will have to wait until we meet. We need to meet as soon as possible."

"I don't have my appointment book to hand," she said, because she couldn't process any of this, and she wasn't yet convinced that it wasn't a hoax. "Leave me your name and number, and I'll call you tomorrow."

She quickly pulled out her little black address book and pen and took down his details.

"Do call me as soon as you can. This is a matter of great urgency."

"I'll call you tomorrow."

She hung up, and wasn't any the wiser as to whether this was a hoax call or not. She didn't know what to make of it, but all would be put to right once she called this man back tomorrow and determined that he was a fake.

She walked back inside the town hall, located Francine in the rows of people sitting facing the stage then tiptoed up to her and slid into the seat next to her.

Reed Knight was talking about the new movie theater. Shay couldn't take in any of what he said because she couldn't get over the phone conversation with the lawyer.

"Talking to Blake Kennedy?" Francine whispered, with a grin.

"Huh?" Shay was still dazed. Even when the next keynote speaker went up, she found herself not able to pay any attention. "I'm going back out," she said, becoming increasingly restless.

She walked back out of the room, and took in a few deep breaths of air. It was entirely possible that she had choked on the banana and died and gone to heaven. Only in heaven would she have heard the type of news that Frank Barclay had told her.

Otherwise her life was normal. Average. Boring. Exciting things happened to her friends, like Jenna.

Not to someone like her.

She remained outside until the meeting ended. The socializing part of the evening restarted, where everyone had refreshments and networked. She was about to venture back inside when Blake Kennedy walked out, almost bumping into her. "Are you okay?" he asked.

"I'm fine."

"Only you left the room, and I wondered…"

"I'm fine, thanks."

He seemed to peer at her, as if he didn't really believe her. "Blake, I'm fine. I really am," she insisted, when his gray eyes bore into hers again, only they looked a little blue now. Why had she never noticed his eyes before? Or how dark his hair was?

"What's wrong with you today?" Francine asked, coming over.

"She choked on a banana," Blake told her, then with that annoying grin of his, added, "But I saved her life."

Francine turned to her. "Choked on a banana? That's a first."

"He startled me," Shay cried defensively.

"Typical," said Blake, "She's blaming me when I saved her life." He and Francine laughed, even though Shay didn't think this was funny.

"I need to go. Problems to resolve at the factory. I'll see you ladies next time," he said, eyeing Shay just before he turned to leave.

"When are you going to put that poor man out of his misery?" Francine asked when the man was thankfully out of earshot.

Shay's eyes narrowed. Her nostrils flared.

"Don't pretend you've never noticed?" Francine cried. "That man likes you."

"We don't have that sort of chemistry, and he doesn't think of me like that."

"He would if you expressed an interest in him," Francine threw back.

Blake Kennedy? Shay didn't see it. Maybe she'd been too engrossed in her silent-worship-from-afar of Rourke Halloran to ever notice Blake. The two of them had always talked, but there had never been any bit of attraction between them.

Though he had surprised her slightly tonight, and more so when he had escorted her outside to recover.

It was Rourke she'd always looked forward to seeing, not Blake Kennedy. Rourke was drop-dead gorgeousness, where Blake was rugged and had a coarseness about him. Blake was big, he had big hands—which she'd felt on her body today—and a big frame, where Rourke was suited and charming. Blake was nearly always dressed in lumberjack shirts and jeans, unless he'd come from a business meeting, whereas Rourke was always suited and professional-looking.

And even though she could no longer crush on Rourke Halloran, Blake Kennedy was nothing in comparison.

CHAPTER 6

"What did the recruitment ladies say about the temporary maternity cover?" asked Ralph, as he walked in carrying his helmet.

Blake looked up. "I didn't get the chance to speak to anyone about that."

"Wasn't that the main reason for you going to the meeting?" Ralph broke out into a smile. "Apart from getting a chance to talk to Shay Donovan."

"About that." Blake sat back, and abandoned the paperwork he'd been going through. "I didn't get a chance to speak to either of them about that."

"She wasn't there?"

"Oh she was there." Blake's lips curled up in a smile at the incident. "But she...uh… she choked on a banana."

Ralph's face creased into lines as if this didn't make any sense. "She what?"

"She choked on a banana, and I was nearby, so I gave her the Heimlich maneuver, and saved her life."

Ralph's eyes widened. "The Heimlich, huh? At least you got to put your arms around her." He slapped his thigh in laughter.

"I pray you never have to perform that on anyone."

"Shame you couldn't give her the kiss of life," Ralph continued, wiping his eyes because he'd laughed so much. "That's the only way you're ever going to have the balls to kiss her."

"I don't know where you're getting these ideas from," Blake said. Shay had visited the factory early last year which was why Ralph noticed her and remembered her. He had caught Shay and Blake laughing about something, and because these things were rare—Blake being in the company of a woman, and laughing with her—Ralph had always assumed he had a thing for her.

"Someone's got to remind you that there's more to life, otherwise you're likely to die at your desk."

"Thanks," Blake muttered. "Nice to know that you're so worried about my well-being."

"But the Heimlich," said Ralph, nodding his head in what looked like semi-approval. "You went behind her and put your arms around her, then pumped her?"

"It wasn't quite like that."

Ralph chortled. "I'm joking with you."

"It could have been fatal."

"You saved her life," Ralph stated, "I hope she remembers that. At least it's a start."

"A start to what?"

"That woman noticing you. Otherwise you're a lost cause."

"Yeah, yeah." Blake feigned a loud yawn. "Meeting women is the last thing on my radar." Blake folded his arms, getting defensive. "It's because I have no idea about anything else but the business that I can afford to pay everybody and increase their salary year on year—something that a lot of new business owners do not do. So consider yourself lucky, my friend. Shouldn't you be on the factory floor, keeping an eye on things?"

Ralph slipped his helmet back on his head. "Noted." And then he left. Ralph was more than a foreman; he was someone who Blake increasingly relied on to run his ideas and business moves by. The guy was older, and had so many years' worth of experience, Blake often learned from him more than he cared to admit.

But he did need to sort out the maternity leave cover. Maybe he'd wait until the next meeting in a month's time. Or he could call Shay now and find out if she was alright. She was alright, he was certain of that, but he could call and find out, and ask about the maternity cover now. It would give him an excuse to talk to her about something. He wouldn't usually care, but he'd managed to spend more time with her than usual yesterday, and this morning Shay was on his mind.

As for Ralph and his hare-brained idea, it was just that; hare-brained. Shay was cute, intelligent, and funny, but he wasn't sure if she was single or not. He'd never been able to figure it out. It wasn't the type of question he could easily slip into a business conversation, and most of their conversations and dealings tended to be around his business, or her work.

He didn't know her that well, and not at all in a personal manner.

CHAPTER 7

Shay was desperate to call the lawyer and to prove that it had been a hoax call, but she didn't get a moment to herself all morning. So, during her lunch break she walked over to Books & Buns, the bookshop that was a good twenty minute walk away, in order to get a sandwich and make her call.

She found a table away from the serving counter and dialed the number she'd noted down.

When a woman answered, Shay explained the nature of her call.

"Putting you through," she said, not even giving Shay enough time to process that this wasn't a hoax; this was real—the lawyer, and his office, and therefore, the will.

"Miss Donovan, I was waiting for your call."

"Sorry, I was busy all morning."

"Do you believe me now, Miss Donovan? I was under the impression that you didn't quite believe me when we spoke yesterday."

Did she believe him?

No.

Yes.

She didn't know. "It seems a little more real," she confessed.

"Good. Because this is all very, very real, I assure you. We need to meet in person to discuss everything. I am prepared to fly out today."

"Fly out where?"

"To see you, of course. Regarding the matter of your Great Aunt Dena's will."

"But I've never met her," Shay blurted out. "It doesn't make sense why she would pick me."

"Who knows what goes through some people's minds when they make decisions about who to leave their legacies to?"

"But she didn't even know me. And I didn't know much about her. All I know is that her husband died after they got married, and after that my Great Aunt languished into some kind of depression." From what she remembered her mom telling her, it wasn't quite of Miss Haversham proportions; she didn't stay dressed in her wedding dress and keep the wedding cake in her house, as Charles Dickens' lonely character had, but she never remarried. She spent her days pining for her dead husband.

"She was estranged and eccentric, from what I understand. And she didn't leave *everything* to you, Miss Donovan. She left a quarter of her entire fortune to one of the cat sanctuaries here in Savannah."

"She did?"

A quarter?

"A quarter of what?" she asked.

"I'm afraid I can't tell you. Is tomorrow morning convenient for you?" the lawyer asked.

"For what?" Her mind was still on her Great Aunt Dena and the tragedy of her life. Her mother hadn't spoken much of her, and apart from knowing that she cut off ties with the family, and lived a reclusive life after her husband died.

"To meet, Miss Donovan. There are stipulations to your Great

Aunt's will, and her estate is considerable. As I mentioned earlier, I am happy to come over to you, or alternatively, you are more than welcome to come over here. Our offices are in Savannah."

Shay huffed out an indignant breath. "I can't fly to Savannah!" She barely had time to do anything other than work or be there for her parents.

"Then I shall come to you."

"You're actually coming here? To see me?"

"I completely understand your bewilderment, Miss Donovan, but I need to prepare you. This is nothing compared to what I have to tell you regarding your great aunts' will. You can be assured of that. I plan to fly out tonight, and I will be in Starling Bay tomorrow. I shall be staying at The Grand Hotel. I trust that we can meet tomorrow?"

"Well, if you're flying there tonight, it would be rude of me not to meet you."

"Shall we say ten o'clock tomorrow?"

"Yes," she said, and then hung up.

Great Aunt Dena had left a considerable estate, with a quarter going to the cat sanctuary, and the rest to her.

This could not be real.

CHAPTER 8

She canceled her evening meet-up with Jenna and postponed it to the following week. She was having trouble concentrating at work after she returned from the bookshop, and after the conversation with the lawyer.

Later that night she went to bed thinking that Frank Barclay had probably landed and was staying at The Grand Hotel, and that she was going to see him tomorrow. Why the rush? What did he mean when he said there was no time to waste?

Sleep did not come easy and, for a change, it was due to something that might be positive—for she still didn't know what to make of the lawyer's words until she met him. Usually, when she tossed and turned it was because of worrying about her dad.

The next morning she finally crawled into work looking like death.

It didn't help that she had a post-it note stuck on her computer screen telling her that Blake Kennedy had called, and could she call him back? She whipped the note off and tossed it to the side. That man likely wanted to laugh at her about her banana choking incident, but she had far weightier matters to tend to.

Frank Barclay

At ten o'clock, she was in the lobby of The Grand Hotel to meet a man she had never seen before. She looked around, feeling foolish, and she prayed that she would not run into someone she knew here because she wouldn't be able to explain what she was doing hanging around here and waiting for someone. She was the only single person standing impatiently near the sofas.

As it turned out, the hotel was relatively quiet. Only couples and families with young children were around. She assumed that many were on vacation.

As she glanced around, she saw a middle-aged man who appeared to fit the description of an attorney well. He was sitting on the sofa at the furthest end of the lobby area. There was a shiny black leather briefcase lying on the small coffee table in front of him, he was dressed in a dark blue suit and wearing a waistcoat that was obviously too tight. He looked up and caught her staring at him.

When she smiled, he got up and walked over to her.

"Shay Donovan?" he asked.

She nodded, and put out her hand. "Frank Barclay," he announced and shook her hand. Then he pulled out his business card and gave it to her. "In case you need further proof because I assume this is still very unreal to you right now."

He wasn't wrong. "You have no idea." She glanced at the business card before sliding it into her jacket pocket.

He looked around. "It's a shame we don't have an office because what I have to tell you is very important, and it's not for anyone else's ears."

"You're in Starling Bay," she said, "nobody knows you're here. You could be a KGB spy for all it mattered."

He smiled.

She wanted to get this over with so that she could return to work. "I can't imagine what you would have to tell me that would matter much to anybody else."

"Let's sit down and get on with this then, shall we? I have a flight to catch late in the afternoon."

Since it was only just past ten in the morning, she was sure they had plenty of time and that he was in no danger of missing his flight.

She followed him back to where he had been sitting, away from the bar area and the hotel entrance, and tucked away in an alcove in the corner.

Shay didn't have a clue as to what to expect. She'd tried to prepare herself. There was an inheritance, and it seemed that a sum of money had been left to her. Beyond that, though, she had no idea, especially with regards to his references about time.

The lawyer set out his paperwork and handed over some papers to her. "This is a copy of the will. You can read it now, or at your leisure, but I'm going to go through it with you here."

Shay sat back and glanced at it, but it was written in legal language, and she was already feeling nervous. She couldn't follow it, and she couldn't relax. She sat forward, then crossed her legs, then smoothed down her skirt, then clasped her hands together, but she still wasn't comfortable. His manner of talking, and his demeanor, told her that he was about to drop something big on her; he had alluded to as much in the phone call and the fact that he had flown over so fast added to her feeling of anxiety. She had considered asking her mom to be here, but she knew her mother had other things to worry about and Shay didn't want to burden her with anything else until she knew what this man had to say.

"Your Great Aunt was a wealthy woman in her own right. The man she married, who unfortunately died a few weeks after their wedding day, was also a rich Englishman."

"How many weeks after?" Shay asked, because, presumably, this man knew more than anyone in her family had told her. She wasn't even sure her mother knew everything.

"Three weeks after."

"Three?" She had no idea it had been that soon. "What happened?"

"You don't know?" he asked.

"I didn't know her. She might as well have been a stranger to me, which is why I don't understand why she would leave me her inheritance."

"According to the letters left behind, explaining the reason for her will, it's because she had nobody else to leave it to. She met her fiancé when she traveled to England with her parents. They were engaged within months, by the time she returned to the US. He wanted to get married then, but she wanted to wait. They wrote to one another, and then he persuaded her to return and marry him because there was the threat of war looming."

"War?"

He nodded. "So she returned to England a year later, and they married quickly because he was getting deployed imminently. He was a soldier in the British Army, you see. As it turned out, he was deployed the same day."

Shay's mouth fell open.

"Unfortunately, he died weeks later. They had never consummated their marriage."

A breath escaped from Shay's mouth. "Your aunt returned to the US, and stayed here. Edward Jeffreys was an only child, and his fortune, upon his parents' death, also passed to him, and through his death, to his widow. Further, the wealth your Great Aunt amassed during her lifetime grew far beyond anybody's expectations. She now has a net worth of twenty-eight million dollars, and she—"

"How much?"

He lowered his voice. "Twenty-eight million dollars."

Shay's body went limp. Her stomach bottomed out.

"It's remarkable really," the lawyer continued, as calm as

anything. "Because this wasn't the result of any business, as such. Her parents had money, and so did his, but nothing like this. This wealth your Great Aunt acquired from a shrewd mind, and investing in shares and businesses, and in her dying months, she cashed it all out. This is the sum of her life's work."

"She was a recluse," Shay murmured, remembering another detail that her mother had told her.

"That may be, but she was obviously of sound mind, even if her heart was broken."

"Twenty-eight million dollars," Shay repeated, shocked. She couldn't imagine what one million dollars would look like, let alone twenty-eight of them.

"Your Great Aunt decreed that a quarter of her estate be donated to the cat sanctuary which was set up in her name in Georgia and the remaining three quarters were to go to you."

"To me?" Even though he had told her this yesterday, she still couldn't quite believe it. And she believed it even less now that he'd been spitting these kinds of numbers at her.

"Yes, you, Shay Donovan."

Three quarters of twenty-eight million dollars?

"Twenty-one million dollars, Miss Donovan."

She was grateful that he had spelled it out for her.

"Twenty-one million…" The words trailed to a whisper.

"And the cats did well out of it, too."

It still didn't make any sense.

Twenty-one million dollars? For her?

"But why me?" It didn't seem right, especially when she had never even spoken to her. This was an insane amount of money to be leaving to a complete stranger.

"I wish I could ask her but your Great Aunt is no longer here so we shall never know."

"But there were other children and other family members, surely? Even on her husband's side?"

"No. Her husband was an only child, and your aunt was an only child. There were no children." He looked away. "And since they weren't even able to consummate the marriage…"

Shay let those words sink in. She fanned her face because it was too much to take in.

"However, there are two stipulations." He cleared his throat. "She wants to leave it the money to you on the condition that you are happily married, or about to be married."

"Happily married?" Shay almost jumped out of her seat. She placed her hands on the couch on either side of her. "Or about to be married?" This was insane.

"Properly, and happily married, yes, or about to be. And you stand to get the inheritance after your first married year."

She spluttered in indignation. "First married year?"

"Your aunt died heart broken, and she had suffered what she considered to be the cruellest of fates, that she and her husband married but were never able to spend their married life together. She never got over the pain of him being killed shortly after they took their vows. She lived her life imagining what it would be like to have had him alive and by her side. And her dying wish was to leave her money to you, because you are the only woman of marriageable age on her side of the family. She was most particular about leaving the money to a female member, and she wants you to enjoy the money but to enjoy it and share it with the love of your life.

But I haven't met the love of my life. This was getting stranger and stranger. "But I'm not happily married," Shay retorted.

"No, but your great aunt obviously assumed you might be in a relationship and that you, being of marriageable age, might have been engaged, or be getting ready to settle down soon."

Shay puffed out a shocked breath. She hadn't had a boyfriend in a while, and she had no one in the running. Rourke was a fantasy crush who now had a new girlfriend.

It left nobody.

But, twenty-one million dollars was not to be laughed at.

Or ignored.

It was life-changing money indeed. It would mean that she could move into an apartment that wasn't infested with spiders. It would mean that she could move into something bigger, and luxurious. It would mean she could stop working and go traveling instead.

But, more than that, it would mean she could get her father the best healthcare and pay all of his medical bills without worry.

There were a million things she could do with that amount of money, the possibilities were limitless. She really had no idea what she could do because she'd never been faced with this kind of situation before.

This was real.

And it was happening to her.

How could she turn away this once in a lifetime opportunity?

"I'm not married… yet," she said, and wondered where the 'yet' had come from. "But we were talking about getting engaged."

The lawyer looked at her hand, and her ring finger.

"Not that I could wear a ring because I'm allergic to metal," she said, quickly.

"Allergic to metal?"

"To platinum, and silver and gold." She laughed. "It's been difficult deciding on an engagement ring, and so we keep putting it off."

The lawyer pressed his lips together and nodded. "While you don't need to be married right now, Miss Donovan, the clock starts ticking as of today, as of the date I've given you this will and you've signed to indicate that you've understood everything —"

"The clock starts ticking for what?"

"For you to get married."

"To… to get married?"

"You have a month as of now in which to get married. Right now would be ideal."

"Ideal?" *And right now?*

"Twenty-one million dollars is a lot of money to go to a cat sanctuary, Miss Donovan, and if you are already engaged, I'd advise you to get married now, so that you are within the one month date in order to comply with the requirements of the will."

She blinked, unsure as to what he was advising her. Surely, he wasn't supposed to advise her? Surely not in this way? "Do you have any questions, Miss Donovan?"

Did she have any questions? Heck yes. Marriage had been the last thing on her mind, *ever*. Great Aunt Dena was a name she'd heard of a handful of times in her entire life, and she didn't have a boyfriend. She had no 'body' to marry. "I don't fully understand the time clause."

"It's really very simple."

"I'm easily confused."

"I'm just saying that if you and your boyfriend are ..ahem—" He cleared his throat, "engaged, or about to get engaged, that you hurry it up and get married now so that you can be sure to comply with the rules of the will."

She stared at him, momentarily speechless, before asking, "Is that the only way."

"It's the only way. Of course, if you were single, I would tell you there is no way you would receive the inheritance. You see, your aunt had a huge regret that she didn't get married soon after she got engaged. As a result, she was always pre-occupied by time, simply because she feels she wasted that year. In the end she only had a few hours after marrying her husband. She regrets that. One can only suppose that it was a lesson she learned only too late. She had regrets, and she doesn't want her beneficiary to have the same."

The whole thing was insanely, ridiculously mad.

He grinned, a hawkish, pointed grin that had no real warmth to it. "You have to be already married or married within one month on from this date, and further, you need to stay married for one year before you are entitled to receive the money."

"And what if we ... if we decide to divorce after a year?"

"Then you are free to do so."

"And the money?"

"You will receive one million dollars. The rest will go to the cat sanctuary."

"One million?" This was a number she could envision a little more easily than the twenty-one million. It was a big drop, but to her, one million dollars was still huge. It was still life-changing money, and it would help with her father's medical expenses. This type of windfall wasn't to be sniffed at.

Her mind began working overtime. She wouldn't come into any money for a year, but if she stuck it out for a year, she would be rich. Even if she divorced, she would still have more money than she had to her name today.

It wasn't just the money, but her mind was drawn to all the things that money could buy, what having that much money would mean for her father. The peace of mind it would give her parents.

The only problem was she had to find a man out of thin air.

"According to her letters, your Great Aunt had already considered that if you were in a relationship and happy with somebody, why would you wait the way she had? She's only helping you to make your mind up sooner or not as a case may be."

"I understand how life changing and completely overwhelming this must be for you, Miss Donovan. If you need more time to think about it, that's perfectly fine, but time is of the essence."

"I only receive the money at the end of the year?"

"That's right."

"Of course, you are also free to say that you are not in a position to get married so soon, and if that is the case, I'm sure the cat sanctuary will benefit greatly from it."

"I need some time to … to discuss these matters with my … my … partner."

"You have a lot to think about. In the meantime, I have some paperwork for you to sign, to say that you have understood the terms of your great aunt's will and that, should you agree to get married, then we can set the process in motion. Of course, we will need to see a marriage certificate, and, your Great Aunt, ever the eccentric, also stipulated that someone from my office will be able to turn up to check on you."

"Whatever for?"

"To make sure that you are married and that there is nothing fraudulent about this claim."

Shay forced a smile.

"Your Great Aunt wanted her estate to go to the right person, not someone who was going to twist the rules of the will in order to get the money. Not that I foresee you doing anything like that."

Shay smiled at him weakly.

"You and your boyfriend have been together a while now?"

The image of Blake Kennedy suddenly flashed through her mind. She lowered her head and warbled a weak, "Yes. We have."

"How long?"

She tried to think back to how long she had seen him at the town hall meetings. "Two, maybe three years?"

The lawyer's face twisted. "Which is it?"

"Three."

She couldn't believe she was doing this. Lying to the lawyer in the name of getting her paws on her Great Aunt Dena's fortune.

Oh, but the cats wouldn't need any more money, she told herself. They already had plenty to be happily meowing about.

She smiled and placed her hands on her lap. "He's a lovely guy. *Lovely*. We've been talking about getting married recently…"

He nodded. "Could you sign here, here and here please." He put a form in front of her and showed where she needed to sign. "This is to show that you have acknowledged and understood everything I've told you."

She looked at him as if everything he had explained to her had been completely erased from her memory. He smiled revealing wrinkles that formed deep on either side of his lips. "If you decide to move your marriage plans forward, we'll be delighted to receive a copy of the wedding certificate and your marital address."

Marital address?

She stared at him in silent shock.

"So that we can turn up and do spot checks to verify the validity of the marriage."

She laughed in disbelief, injected a small amount of indignation into her laugh.

"Of course, I can't imagine you would do anything illegal, but you have to understand that we are simply following your aunt's instructions."

She nodded. All she could think of was her lie. What would she do? How would she ever pull this off?

You don't need to pull this off, she reminded herself. Tell him you are single and have no one in mind. You've not dated in over a year, and you have no intention of doing so just to get the inheritance.

Blake Kennedy saved your life. Maybe you could pay him back.

This last thought was hard to shake off.

What was it that Francine had said to her? *That man likes you.*

She could reward him handsomely.

"I think you have more than enough to consider. It was good to meet you, Miss Donovan. I trust we may or may not hear from you again, in the next month. Good luck with the wedding," he cleared his throat again, "In the event that you decide to bring your wedding forward."

She couldn't believe that the mention of so much money had made her lie so easily, that her mind was already looking for a way in which she could pull this off.

"Thank you."

She was an honest person, had never done anything illegal, or committed a wrong act. Had never sworn, or lied...much.

But, twenty-one million dollars wasn't easy to ignore, neither was one million. This was temptation staring her right in her face.

The cats really didn't need any more millions, but they would, no doubt, end up with the bulk of Aunt Dena's inheritance.

Somehow, her brain was already working out ways in which she could fit the will and make it work for her. She didn't need much. She would be happy with one million.

She remained seated on the comfy couch in the lobby, once Frank Barclay left, and she went over everything that he had just told her.

This type of stuff only happened in books and films. This didn't happen to real people in real life.

A month.

Her Great Aunt Dena had been clever. She'd left a short interval of time so that people wouldn't be looking for a partner with the sole intention of inheriting her money.

But this was exactly what Shay was thinking of doing.

She had a month in which to get married.

Which meant she needed to find a man to marry in the next few weeks.

She decided she wouldn't tell her pretend-husband the reason why she needed the money. She wouldn't want him to feel trapped, or guilty, in case he couldn't handle it and wanted to leave.

It also meant she couldn't tell her friends about her sudden marriage. Or her parents. They could never know she married for the money. She had told them that she'd had a promotion at work and that was how she could afford to help them with their medical bills. Ordinarily she was an honest girl, but she already lied to her parents because she wanted to help them.

But, what would Jenna say? Or Francine?

She froze at the thought of the on-the-spot checks.

It meant she would need to live with someone.

And who did she know well enough to let into her apartment? Nobody.

She pinched herself, and looked at her watch when her phone rang. It was the receptionist. "Francine's asking where you are."

"I'm… I'm… I had some personal matters to take care of. I'm on my way back now."

"I'll let her know. By the way, did you call Blake Kennedy? I left a note on your screen."

"I got it, and no, I didn't call him."

Blake Kennedy.

Francine's words rang in her ears.

That man likes you.

Blake Kennedy.

Oh, dear god.

What was she doing even entertaining this thought?

CHAPTER 9

"Are you sure, sweetie? That's a lot of money."

"I'm sure, Mom." She forced a laugh so that her mother wouldn't worry about the money she didn't have. About the loan she had taken out, on the pretense that she was buying a car, but using it to help out with her parents. She had seven thousand dollars put away in the bank, and had told herself she would pay her parents as and when they asked for it rather than paying the entire sum. It gave her peace of mind to know that she had that much money to her name.

"It's another five hundred dollars."

"That's fine, Mom. I've got this. Don't you worry. I'll transfer it over as soon as I get home."

"Thanks, sweetie. Come and visit when you can. Your father's feeling rather weak at the moment. You always perk him up"

"Don't worry, Mom. I'll come."

She hung up. Her father had had a lobectomy where they had cut out the cancer in a part of his lung. The surgery had been successful but he now needed four chemo cycles in the next four to six months to completely kill the cancer. It meant that her mother had to take a lot of time off work in order to care for her father. Shay tried to visit them most weekends.

The health bills were mounting. Shay set an alarm on her phone so that she could do the bank transfer at home. She always felt paranoid about doing these things on her cell phone or from the work computer.

If she had been toying before with the idea of fulfilling Great Aunt Dena's criteria for the inheritance, she was now seriously contemplating it now.

The huge glaring problem was that she needed a man. She had a month in which to find him and marry him.

Focus on the equation, she told herself; the one that stated:

Marriage + one year of living with a stranger = one million dollars.

She coached herself to breathe slowly in order to calm herself down.

The very idea of finding a man brought her out in panic.

Focus on the equation.

If she applied her usual logical and reasoning, and ignored the emotion, and her heart, she could do it.

It made sense.

The money was not only life-changing, it had the potential to be *life-saving.*

Her father could get the best treatment that money could buy.

The very best.

And she could pay it without having a heart attack herself.

It seemed that every few days her mother talked about this test, or that test. The seven thousand dollars was going to disappear fast at this rate.

Blake Kennedy. The name bubbled up every few hours. Maybe he was the solution to the problem Great Aunt Dena had created for her.

She didn't mean to be ungrateful, and that was a crazy sum of money, but did she really need to put her through these hoops and obstacles in order to get it?

Of course, if she had been in Jenna's place, if she had already met and fallen head over heels in love with someone, then this would be an easy problem to solve.

Trying to find a man she had to convince to marry her, and live with her for a year—this was the huge problem she could not see a way around.

She had briefly considered using dating websites to find a partner but she had never tried these things before and really didn't want to try them now. Besides, finding total strangers was risky, and psychos and murderers would be hard to spot.

She didn't want to die trying to gain the inheritance.

Which kind of only left Blake Kennedy.

Or Rufus Wilson from work. He was the only single guy at work and she had known him for years.

He was also fifteen years older than her and had bad breath.

Not that she had any intentions of doing anything with him.

But still, if the man was going to live in her apartment—and she had already decided they would live there—she would feel a little better if it was someone she knew.

She walked past the photocopier where Rufus was standing and smiled at him as he walked past.

"Hey," he said. She glanced at his potbelly and his receding hairline. There was no way in heaven, no way on earth even, that she would let that man into her apartment, on the pretense of a fake marriage.

No way at all.

Which left Blake Kennedy as the only other possible alternative.

Only, she didn't want to think about it now. She'd think about it later because she was meeting Jenna tonight at her new apartment. Her friend had moved twice since leaving Shay's apartment. First she'd found her own place, and then Reed had convinced her to move into one of his many properties because he felt it would be 'nicer' for her.

But, she could give Blake a call. After all, he'd called her, hadn't he? A few days ago, and she'd simply forgotten about it.

Faulty machinery?

More costs.

Blake stared at his foreman in dismay.

"Just letting you know," said Ralph. "That's the second time in two months we've had to call someone out to fix it."

"I'll see what I can do, thanks for the update."

He slammed his pen down on the table. He didn't need this on top of everything else. He tried to do everything right: train his staff, invest in their futures, expand the manufacturing plant, have the most up-to-date machinery.

Only, he'd hoped that the machines would have been more resilient.

This was another headache he could do without.

When the phone rang, he looked at it and was in no mood to answer it.

"It's Shay Donovan," said Nancy. "Putting her through."

"Hello," he said, barked more like it, because the monetary costs were still ringing through his head.

"Have I caught you at a bad time?" she asked, obviously noticing his tone.

He sat back, his nerves slowly de-frazzling from the sound of her voice. "No, no. You caught me off guard. What can I do for you?"

"Uh... I'm not sure," she replied, sounding surprisingly upbeat. "You called me."

"That was a few days ago," he said. "And you're calling me back only now?" He was obviously further down on her list of important people.

"Yes."

"What if it had been an urgent matter?" he asked, starting to smile.

"I'm assuming you would have called the next day."

"I guess I should be thankful that you remembered to call at all?" He had only called her out of courtesy the day after the town hall saga, to find out how she was because that was the type of guy he was, but now that they were getting back to their usual banter, he wasn't about to own up to it. "I meant to talk to you the other day about getting some temporary maternity cover staff," he said, quickly thinking off the top of his head.

"Maternity cover?"

"That's right. I meant to speak to you or Francine about it the other night but events overtook us."

"I see. Of course we can find you the right staff. When do you need them for, and how many?"

"Three."

"You have three women leaving to have babies at the same time?"

"Around Christmas," he told her. "That would be pretty good commission for you, right?"

"It would be, yes."

"Anyway, that was the reason for my call," he lied. Still, it was great to hear from her, and she was a good distraction from the costly repairs he'd been looking into.

"We can definitely help you."

"It's not urgent," he hastened to add. "I was going to talk to you about it at the next meeting in the town hall."

"But you called me about it so..."

"I did." The main reason had been nothing do with the

maternity cover but now that he'd told one white lie he had to follow it up with other white lies.

"How about we meet up?" she asked, suddenly, throwing him for a loop.

"Meet up?"

"Meet up as in get together and talk about it," she suggested.

For something that wasn't going to become urgent until the end of the year? What was going on? He was lucky if he ever got more than a few sentences out of Shay on a good day, and a few sarcastic sentences at that. That was mostly how they related to one another. He liked their conversations, but this was something else, something unusual.

He realized she was waiting for his reply, and that he hadn't yet given one.

"You did save my life, and I figure I could make it up to you," she said.

Huh?

This was most bizarre. "Uh... sure," he replied, still wondering how the Heimlich maneuver had changed their dynamics so much.

"How about lunch one day?" she suggested. "I could come over to your factory?"

"I don't have much free time during the working day," he told her. In addition, he didn't want Ralph skulking around with a huge grin on his face seeing Shay in his office.

"Well then, how about we meet one evening?"

She was really surprising him today, and being so chatty and so eager to see him.

"What did you have in mind?" He didn't know what to make of this.

"How about I buy you dinner one evening?"

"Dinner?"

"Or we could go for drinks at The Grand Hotel, or have a bite to eat at The Olive Tree, or somewhere else, if you'd prefer?"

"A bite to eat?" he murmured, half in surprise. Maybe she was eager to get the commission for the three staff? This change in behavior was totally out of character for Shay. She had never been rude, had never ignored him; they had always spoken, just not like *this*. "Sure," he replied, with certainty. It was better to take her offer now while she was making it. "The Olive Tree sounds fine."

"Great. We'll meet there and you can tell me all about the maternity cover you're looking for."

"Great," he echoed, and then she hung up, which he thought was slightly premature. They'd been having an interesting conversation, and she'd cut it short all of a sudden.

Shay hung up.

In fact, she couldn't put the receiver down fast enough.

She couldn't believe what she had done this; asked Blake Kennedy out on a date.

Only, it wasn't a date so much as...as... a means to ensnare him.

Sort of.

The guy wanted temporary replacement staff. She could have discussed this on the phone.

And he didn't need anyone until Christmas time.

What was she thinking?

One million dollars, that's what.

She had asked him to meet her, but they hadn't fixed a time or a day, and she didn't have time to waste. She immediately called him back. "We didn't decide on the day," she confessed, feeling sheepish.

"No, we didn't," he replied. "I'm free tonight."

She was meeting Jenna at her apartment tonight. "I can't tonight. How about tomorrow?"

"I'm afraid I can't tomorrow."

Her heart sank. "How about next week?"

"I'm away on a business trip."

"You are?" This was bad news.

"How about Friday?" he suggested. "I'll be back by then."

Next Friday? "That's too late," she blurted, in shock.

"Too late for what?"

She'd slipped up. "Did I say too late? I meant that's so great."

"Meeting on Friday?"

"Better late than never."

"Great. See you next Friday."

"I'm looking forward to it," she told him, before hanging up for the second time.

She was going to lose almost a week of time. Which meant that she had to make up her mind fast, depending on what she thought of him, and, depending on whether he agreed to her crazy idea.

At least now she not only had a date, a place and time to meet with Blake Kennedy, she had a viable reason for the meeting. And, if she had the courage, and possibly enough white wine, she might be brave enough to put the question to him.

"How about we get married for a year, and you'll get half a million dollars at the end of it?"

What would he make of that?

CHAPTER 10

"This is beautiful!" Shay squealed. "How can you afford this place? It's huge, and it's gorgeous. Shay's eyes widened in amazement at Jenna's apartment in Forest Heights.

Oh, how the tables had turned. It seemed like only a few months ago that Jenna had come to Starling Bay with not more than a few dollars to her name.

"It's not mine," said Jenna. "It's one of Reed's many properties. Olivia used to live here."

Shay made a face at the mention of that name.

"Well, it's yours now. You live here."

"But it's still not mine," Jenna insisted. "And, I pay him rent for it. He wouldn't take it at first, but I insisted."

But Shay had drifted off and was admiring the apartment, the huge windows, and the gorgeous view overlooking Lake Ivanhoe and the woods. The expensive looking furniture, state-of-art flat screen TVs and kitchen and appliances.

And all she could think of was her own dingy little apartment.

"I love this place," she sighed, more with envy, than anything else. This was what plenty of money could buy.

This was what she could buy, if she went along with her aunt's will.

If she, by some fluke chance, managed to convince Blake Kennedy.

Maybe she could do this.

It would mean being able to afford anything she wanted, and it would benefit both of them.

She considered giving him half because it was the first thing that came to her mind, and because it made sense. She assumed it would be an amount tempting enough for the other party and it seemed fair. Right now it didn't seem like real money and as such she couldn't place a value on it.

After all, would Blake willingly want to spend a year living with her? Would he want to be married to her, assuming he agreed to the deal?

If she couldn't convince Blake, or if he didn't seem a good enough candidate—and she hoped dinner with him would lead her to a conclusion one way or another—then she would have to find someone else fast. But she had no one else. Most of her ex's were married now.

She was breaking out in hives just thinking about it.

"You can have a good look around later," said Jenna, rearranging some plates on the kitchen island.

Shay sat down and admired the table full of canapés that Jenna had put out. Shay looked at them. "You didn't have to go to any trouble." She was touched that her friend had, because these looked mouth wateringly divine.

"I didn't. Cecile made them for me."

"You're still friendly with his cook?"

"Yes! Why would I not be?"

"And his butler?"

Shay recalled Jenna didn't have such a great relationship with Pennington.

"He's growing on me, like mold."

They both burst out laughing.

"Come on then," said Jenna, bringing out a bottle of white wine and two glasses.

Shay picked up a canape and plopped it into her mouth. It was heaven in pastry.

"Let me tell you about Montana," said Jenna. And she did. She told Shay about her recent visit with Reed to his family's ranch in Montana.

"What's the ranch like?" Shay asked.

"Huge. They've got of acres of land and millions of horses. Not millions—"

"Obviously not," said Shay, picking up another canape.

"But lots."

"And his parents? How were they towards you?"

"A bit cold at the start, but really nice once I got to know them. I felt really out of sorts at first and wanted to come back."

"You poor thing," replied Shay, empathizing with her friend. It made her wonder, not that the situation was remotely similar, but if she got married by some weird chance, things would be strange at the beginning. But over time, perhaps as they got to know one another, maybe things wouldn't be so bad, or so difficult.

It was all well and good having her eyes on the prize but she had to get through a year of living with a stranger.

As did he.

"Family matters to Reed. His parents matter to him and though you wouldn't think it, he feels that he owes it to them. He wants everyone to be happy. He told me that it was important that the people closest in his life got on, and so, for his sake, I wanted them to like me."

Maybe this would happen to her and her new husband; assuming he agreed to her proposition.

Shay flinched at the word.

Husband.

"Is it bitter?" Jenna asked her.

"Huh?"

"You made a face." Jenna nodded at the canape in her hands.

"Oh, no. This is lovely. Lovely." She popped it into her mouth.

"So, as I was saying, we got talking. After a while you see a way through to the other person, and after a few days, we warmed to one another. His mom is the nicer one. His dad was the one who was slightly difficult, but if you've lived under the same roof for a while, you kind of make allowances."

Shay nodded absent-mindedly. She was listening to her friend, and was happy for her, but at the same time she was trying to see if there was a lesson she could take away from all this.

"So now we need to find you someone, so that we can start going on double dates," said Jenna enthusiastically.

"Double dates?" Shay moaned. "Why do you need to go double dating with me when you can go out with your new set of friends?" Jenna had spoken of Reed's best friends, Dylan and Rourke and had met up with them a few times.

"They're nice enough, but they're Reed's friends first, and you're my friend for ever, so let's talk about finding you Mr. Right."

"There's nothing to talk about," Shay insisted, even though this was a huge lie. There was so much she could tell her, so much she could confide in her about and get her opinion on, but if she was going to do this crazy wild ridiculous thing with Blake maybe it was better that nobody but she and Blake knew about it.

She was doing this to help her family, and one day she might even be able to move into an apartment like this, hopefully without spiders.

She shuddered. She hadn't even given much thought about the

living arrangements; that was something she pushed to the back of her mind.

The equation, never forget the equation.

Marriage + one year of living with a stranger = one million dollars.

As insane as it was to do this, it would be even more insane *not* to do it.

CHAPTER 11

*S*he was nervous.

She'd brushed her hair, put on lipstick and worn her best dress to work; one that would work well for the evening. Then in the evening she made sure that she was purposely running late so that Blake would already be at The Olive Tree by the time she turned up.

Each day this week had seen her almost cancel the meeting with him. Each time she had talked herself out of following through on this crazy idea of hers, but visiting her parents at the weekend had reminded her of why she was doing this.

Now the night of her dinner with Blake was here, and she couldn't back away now.

She walked in and drew in her breath because he was hard to miss, even in the busy restaurant.

She had made an effort, no doubt about it, but she was slightly annoyed at the sight of him because he looked as if he'd come straight from work; he was still sporting his 5 o'clock shadow. To his defense, he wasn't wearing his usual black and blue checked lumberjack shirt but a plain dark colored one from what she could see. He was sitting on a barstool and stood up as soon as he saw her.

Then he held out his hand, which she shook because this was a business meeting, after all, and they'd never greeted one another in any other way. Still, it was odd to see him outside of the town hall meeting.

"Hello, there," she said, feeling slightly nervous.

He nodded. "I wasn't sure if you were going to show up."

This surprised her. She sat down next to him. "You didn't expect me to show up?"

"I wasn't sure, to be honest," he replied, smoothing a hand through his hair. "I didn't know what to make of your suggestion for us to meet here."

"It is outside of our comfort zone, I guess."

"But, I'm glad we decided to change things up," he said, quickly. "What can I get you?" he asked. She saw that he had a bottle of beer.

What would she have? Even as she stood here, on the pretense of arranging to meet him for recruitment purposes, and knowing that she had another ulterior motive, she found her heart racing. "A glass of white wine. Large."

He looked at her. "Large?"

"It's Friday," she replied, as if that explained the extra large size. "And, actually, I'm changing my mind. I'll have a Mimosa." She was in the mood for cocktails.

"A Mimosa?"

"Yes, please. I'm really glad it's the end of the week," she confessed.

"Me too. I totally understand that Friday feeling."

He raised his hand to summon the server's attention and ordered her drink.

The bar was busy and it was becoming quite noisy.

"Cheers," he said, lifting his bottle when her cocktail arrived. She lifted her glass. "To the end of a Friday," he said.

"To the start of the weekend."

He smiled and set down his beer bottle, and because she had twisted around on her stool, and was facing him sideways, she got to have a good look at his face, at his side profile, while he wasn't directly staring at her. When he turned to look at her, her gaze dropped to his watch because her heart did a funny somersault. He was wearing a huge watch which looked expensive, and Blake usually didn't seem the type of guy to be sporting expensive things. Though she knew his company was expanding fast, and he was doing well.

She quickly took another sip of her cocktail and wondered if she was making herself see these things because she had an agenda.

He must have caught her staring a little longer than necessary because he looked puzzled. "Something wrong?"

"No."

He placed his finger on his face, "Do I have something on my face? A rogue booger, or something?"

She laughed. "No." Obviously he'd caught her checking him out. "It's just that you're not wearing a lumberjack shirt for a change."

"I made an effort," he replied. "This is a business meeting, after all."

"Yes, of course it is." She decided to get the business matters out of the way before she broached the other topic. "Tell me about your pregnant employees."

She listened while he told her. "We've got a few months yet. There's no hurry."

"No, but it takes time to get good people," she replied, making notes while he told her of the skill sets he needed for the temporary staff.

"Great. I'll see what I can find for you," she said, when she had all the information she needed.

Now that that was out of the way, an awkward silence followed. They had discussed the business matter, and really there wasn't that much to discuss, certainly not enough to warrant a meeting like this.

She gulped down her cocktail for courage. "I think I'll get another one," she said, raising her hand to call the server. She glanced at his bottle. It was still half-full. "How about you?"

"I'm fine for now," he replied, easily. "But maybe you need to ..." He stopped himself.

"Need to what?"

"I was going to suggest that you slow down, but I realize that sounds patronizing."

She considered his words, and warmed towards him just-a-little.

When the server came over, she ordered another cocktail.

"Cheers," she said, when he delivered it swiftly. "Here's to us I mean, to our business arrangement, the maternity cover one."

"What other one is there?" he asked, revealing beautiful perfectly straight Hollywood teeth. She hadn't noticed that about him before. How had she not?

"You're not usually so chirpy," he commented.

"You don't usually get to see the other side of me. At the town hall meetings I'm on my best behavior."

"Is that right?" he asked, smiling.

She smiled back. "Yes. I'm happier when it's the end of the week."

"Who isn't?"

"How is business?" she asked, eager to keep the conversation flowing. She listened as he proceeded to tell her about his hefty tax bill, and the increasing manufacturing costs, and the recent problems he'd had with faulty equipment. "But you're insured aren't you?"

"I am, but faulty machinery causes a bottleneck in our manufacturing plant and these things have a ripple effect which causes our output to take a hit. Problems, big or small, always seem to have some sort of effect on my bottom line. Profits will take a hit. And you can imagine how difficult it is managing cash flow in a business. You can do without the extra headaches."

"I bet you wish you won the lottery?"

"That would be the answer to my prayers, but for now I'll have to scale back and hold off on a few things."

"But what if you *did* win the lottery?"

He raised an eyebrow. "If I won the lottery? There's more chance of getting abducted by aliens."

"You'd be surprised," she replied, her tone slightly flirtatious, slightly indignant. She swatted him playfully.

"If I won the lottery, it would fix so many headaches. It would cure a lot of my problems, but since that's never going to happen, I won't dwell on it, because I like to live in the real world most of the time—"

"Most of the time?"

"Yes, most of the time, and I assume you do too. Got to say, Shay, you're surprising me this evening."

She giggled. "But what if you came into money, not through winning the lottery, but through some other means?"

He set down his beer bottle. "Are you planning on robbing a bank or something?"

"Nothing that risky.

He almost choked. "Nothing that risky? What in the devil are you up to?"

She looked around, and then leaned in towards him. "We should go and sit in the corner, away from everyone, because if you're surprised now, you haven't heard the half of it."

His gray eyes widened. "You want to get a table, with me? In the corner?"

"You might want to eat once you've heard me out."

He almost choked in surprise. "I'm intrigued." He raised his hand to attract the server's attention and asked if they had a free table. As it turned out, they were lucky, and there were two free tables. At Shay's suggestion, they took the one that was tucked away in a corner.

CHAPTER 12

his was it.

As she sat across the table from Blake, over a trio of pretty candles flickering in the subdued lighting of the restaurant, the atmosphere seemed almost romantic. An innocent bystander watching them would think she and Blake were a couple in love.

Laughter and chatter rippled in the background, glasses tinkled, and cutlery sounded against porcelain plates. The warm, homey smell of delicious food floated in the air.

Shay had finished her second cocktail, and when the server passed by, she ordered another one.

No sooner had she placed the order, when Blake leaned forward. "Are you sure you want another one?"

"Do you not trust me to have a third cocktail?" She needed it, because she couldn't say what she had to say to him completely sober. She wasn't drunk, but the courage another cocktail would give her would help.

"Are you driving home?" he asked. "I'm worried about how you're getting home."

"I caught a cab here."

"Okay," he replied, seeming somewhat less worried. "I didn't..." he cleared his throat, "I didn't mean to patronize you. You're sensible and I know you can take care of yourself. I don't want you to think that I know better than you."

She opened her mouth to say something, but words temporarily eluded her, instead she looked at him for the longest time. He was a real gentleman. He had shown himself to be worthy of what she was about to put to him because he seemed like the type of guy she could last a year with; more so than Rufus, and she didn't really have anyone else.

"Thanks, I appreciate your concern," she said.

"I mean, this is weird," he said, tapping his finger on the table. "You, me, here. This..." He waved his arm around to indicate the restaurant.

If he thought this was weird, he had no idea what was coming next.

Given their love-hate conversations at the weekly meetings, Blake Kennedy was shaping up to be a real contender for the role of her husband. She needed to tell him.

She'd never seen him in the same way that she had seen Rourke Halloran. Rourke she had always admired from a distance, and Blake...well, they had pretty much ended up talking on every occasion. Their conversations were loaded with dry wit and sarcasm.

Always light, never deep, and they had always gotten on even if their conversations might have sounded prickly to others.

Yet spending this evening with him now had completely opened her eyes. Blake listened, he was attentive, and he seemed caring.

He'd also saved her life the other day.

But was he single?

She sat upright, not having even contemplated his status. For some reason, she wasn't sure why, she had assumed he would be available. She couldn't tell him anything about the will until she had determined his status, and now that they had moved to a table away from the noisy bar, she needed to get to work.

"What's so strange about this?" she asked, trying to contain the beating of her heart. She leaned forward and looked into his dark eyes. They twinkled with something that bordered on concern.

"You," he said. "I'm worried about you. Is something going on?" he shrugged. "Something bothering you?"

"I'm perfectly fine, thank you."

"You're beginning to worry me."

He was handsome. Or maybe it was the drink. He was something like a diamond in the rough. She sat back and stared at his 5 o'clock shadow which he often had. But sitting as she was, not more than a few feet away from him, she was starting to see him with appreciative eyes.

Maybe the third cocktail was helping.

"How do you see me?" she asked, out of the blue, and not knowing how else to phrase the question.

He laughed, then shook his head, then lifted his beer bottle to his lips and took a swig. "You are really starting to worry me."

"But if you could answer the question. I mean," she said, putting down her glass, and running her finger around the base. "We've known one another for three years now."

"Three years and five months."

Holy mackerel. She inhaled a deep breath. "You've been counting the months?"

"No," he replied, setting his beer bottle down and leaning forward. "It's just that I took over the business three and a half years ago, and I kept most of the staff, that's how I acquired my head foreman, Ralph, and his wife, Nancy, she's the office manager. Ralph was the one who told me about the town hall meetings, which I started attending as soon as I could, and I remember you, because I was looking to recruit. That's when I met you and Francine. But I digress. You wanted to know what I thought of you.

"I'm curious to know."

His eyebrows pushed together. "The only impressions I have of you are from those meetings. You're ... hmmm." He seemed momentarily stumped. "Let's see now. I think..." he cleared his throat. "Why are you asking? It makes me feel as if I'm on a blind date."

"Do you go on many?"

"Blind dates?" he asked. "Heck no, even though I'm single, a blind date is the last thing I'd try."

But he'd given her an answer. The plan was still good to go.

"I find you sensible and easy to talk to. Professional, and funny."

"Funny?"

"You can be, sometimes. I can't think of anything right now. I can't pinpoint an exact situation."

She nodded, welcoming the feedback. So far, he hadn't mentioned anything about being attracted to her. But it was all good.

"You're not wearing your glasses today," he stated, as if he'd only now noticed.

"Is this the first time you've seen me without glasses?"

"Yes."

They looked at one another.

She could see he had questions, as well as a huge cloud of confusion swirling around his head.

She couldn't put this off any longer.

"I have something to tell you," she said, "And you must hear me out, and not say a word until I finish.

He looked at her with a really worried look on his face.

"Are you in?"

"Hear me out. I have some financial troubles, nothing more than that, but I'm about to implicate you in something."

He almost choked on his beer. "Am I in trouble?"

"No."

"Promise me you'll listen and not say a word until I've finished?"

"I promise."

"And don't judge me, either."

Now the poor man looked worried. Lowering her voice, she moved forward towards him across the table. "What if there was a once-in-a-lifetime opportunity—" He opened his mouth as if he was about to say something.

"You promised to hear me out without saying a word."

He clamped his lips together. She continued. "A once-in-a-lifetime opportunity where..." She swallowed, finding it difficult to say it, especially with him staring at her like that.

She couldn't say it, so she lowered her gaze.

"Go on," he said, coaxing her.

"If you and I got married and you walked away with half a million dollars, would you do it?" She lifted her eyes to his. "It would be a fake marriage of course, there would be nothing going on and we would lead separate lives. It's not illegal. It's just...not *real*, but at the end of it we stand to make a lot of money and we would both be so much better off financially."

"Is this a scam?"

She lifted her finger, halting him. "You promised to let me finish. I would get some money, and you would get some money, and we wouldn't harm or kill anyone in the process."

His mouth fell open and he raked his hands through his hair. "This doesn't—"

She put her finger to her lips, "All we have to do is agree to get married for a year. We have to get married in the next two weeks. I only found out a few weeks ago and I've been trying to talk myself out of doing this but—"

Blake had gone as white as snow.

"But we need to have the marriage certificate as proof that we got married, and we have to live together because there will be spot checks on us."

"Spot checks?"

She allowed him that. "The lawyers need to know that this is a real marriage."

"But it's not really, it's fake, you said so. What lawyers? What is this, Shay? This is some joke, isn't it? You called me here tonight to play some pranks on me. You had a crazy bet with your friend."

She shook her head.

"You're not joking?" he asked.

"You didn't let me finish."

"Can you blame me?" He took a swig from his beer, and then another one in quick succession.

"I know this is insane. But you can blame my Great Aunt Dena." She proceeded to tell him everything that had happened, how she had found out, how she had met with the lawyer who had flown here.

Everything, except the real, main reason she was doing this; for her father.

"You're asking *me* to marry you?"

"Yes," she replied.

"And you'll be my wife?"

"In name only," she clarified. Her shoulders slumped. Mr. and Mrs. Kennedy. It was the first time she had thought of this. She fanned her face. It was sounding too near, too close to becoming true. Blake hadn't dismissed it, he hadn't told her it was a ridiculous idea.

Her stomach almost bottomed out.

The man was considering her proposal.

Or he was in extreme shock.

"You have to believe that it is as insane for me to say this as it must seem for you to hear it, especially when I don't really know you that well, and we have a love hate relationship at the best of times. But you would get half a million dollars after the year, and I'll show you the legal document, my aunt's will, if you are thinking of considering it"

"Half a million dollars?" he asked.

"That's your share, yes."

"And you're in financial trouble, you said?"

"You could say that. But I am seriously considering this. I could do with the inheritance but I have a problem in that I'm not married, and I don't have a boyfriend—"

"You don't have a boyfriend?"

"No, because if I did I would have asked him, and I don't have anyone else who could potentially be a boyfriend, and Aunt Dena set a time limit of a month—"

"A month? Why a month?"

"So that no one would try to get married just to get the inheritance."

"But that's exactly what you're doing."

"Well, yes. She doesn't know that though because she's dead."

"I see."

"Aunt Dena has left me a fortune, and if I don't get it, it will go to the cat sanctuary in Savannah. She's already left them enough. Think of how much it would help us to have the *money*," she lowered her voice. "Think of what you could do with it for your business."

He seemed to consider it.

"Do you have any questions?" she asked.

"No, but I need another drink."

CHAPTER 13

She wanted him to marry her?

And then he'd get half a million dollars?

It wouldn't be real. There would be no sexy times, nothing.

But they would get married within two weeks, and stay married for a year.

He didn't know who was crazier, her Great Aunt Dena, or Shay.

He'd ordered another bottle of beer after that, and then he understood why Shay had been the way she was this evening.

They'd both remained quiet after that. He had questions. A million of them, but she had told him as much as she knew.

She told him that she still hadn't thought it through properly, and that she had been tying herself up into knots thinking about how to ask him, and that she had at first dismissed the idea, but later had been driven to consider it out of sheer desperation.

She hadn't mentioned much about her financial problems, except to say that the money would help her a great deal.

In the end, the small appetite he had worked up, had vanished.

Shay had felt the same.

They were quiet.

He was thinking.

She looked relieved.

He'd ordered a cab and saw her home, then he went home himself.

Only, he'd woken up yesterday morning with a thundering headache, and when he'd remembered Shay's proposal, it had made his headache even worse.

He hadn't even asked her how much she stood to inherit. As a result he had spent most of the day keeping busy, inspecting the machinery at the factory, which was actually easier to do over the weekend.

But today, there wasn't much to do. The whole time he'd been trying to keep busy, but it had been difficult to concentrate. He kept going over the conversation with Shay.

It would have been better if he'd met up with friends, even friends he seldom called or got in touch with because ever since he'd bought this business, he didn't have time to socialize.

For one brief, crazy moment, he considered calling Ralph, and telling him, but he knew he couldn't tell Ralph, he couldn't even tell his parents or his sister.

In the space of a week or two his life had gone through all kinds of crazy and most of it was Shay's doing.

He stared at his sheet of paper on which he'd scribbled his pros and cons. The pros were that he'd get to help Shay and he'd make a lot of money.

The cons were that it was only a business arrangement, it wasn't exactly legit, and she didn't love him.

But maybe she would come to think of him fondly? Maybe something might come of it. She had spelled out that if they decided to get married there would be boundaries. No sleeping in the same bed, no sexy times, no kissing, no flirting—nothing. He understood that. This was merely a financial arrangement, and they would have to live a lie.

After thinking about it for some time, he reached the same conclusion she had; did the cat sanctuary need the money or did he and Shay?

She wasn't running a business, so he had no idea what her money worries were. Student debt, perhaps?

Overspending on credit cards?

She seemed too sensible and level-headed for that.

He liked her and spending that evening with her had been wonderful, until she'd dropped the bombshell. If anyone had overheard their conversation, they wouldn't have believed what they had heard.

He still couldn't believe what he'd heard.

Nothing about it seemed any saner or any more acceptable today than it had been two days ago.

Could he marry her?

Yes. Easily, even knowing of the circumstances surrounding it, but she didn't seem bothered by it. She had come to him for help, and he was sure she had other people she could have turned to before she came to him, because they were merely acquaintances. The fact that she had turned to him, in light of what she had said about her financial troubles, told him that she had no one else to turn to.

She'd said something about keeping this hidden from everyone else. It was a good idea, and it would make for an easier life for them both.

Neither of them wanted anyone to know they were married. Not parents, or friends, or work colleagues.

Shay was a friend. They'd had a really lovely evening up until the moment she had dropped this ticking time-bomb on him.

He could do it.

She wouldn't suspect that he had always liked her.

And the half a million dollars could fix so many problems for him.

But there was something else at the bottom of all of this; what if during that year he and Shay discovered that they had feelings for one another?

What if she started to feel the same?

That would be as big, if not bigger, than the money.

Heck, yes, he could do this.

He'd made up his mind.

And to hell with the consequences.

He picked up his phone and called her.

CHAPTER 14

*B*lake had called her and asked if they could meet by the sea, near the ice-cream parlor.

This time, unlike the meeting at The Olive Tree, she'd arrived there first, and was pacing around near the wall which separated the beach from the promenade.

She pushed up her spectacles, a common habit from years of wearing them. She had come natural this time, no light touch of makeup, no contact lenses. No cocktail to give her courage.

Just her.

The *real* her; worried, and anxious and nervous.

It was one thing to see Blake in a romantically lit restaurant under the partial ruse of a business meeting, and something else to see him in the cold light of day knowing what she had proposed to him.

She stared at the azure blue sea, because it gave her a feeling of calmness she did not possess.

A light tap on her shoulder made her spin around.

It was Blake. Looking oh-so-good. He'd shaved, too.

And he smelled divine. It was refreshing, like cool mint over a sea breeze.

"Hi," she said, pushing her glasses up again.

"Hey."

"Ice-cream?" he asked.

Her mind was so cluttered with what to say, or whether to call the whole thing off, that his question threw her.

He thumbed behind him. "From Kandinsky's."

She shook her head. "I don't feel like eating ice-cream right now." Ice-cream was the last thing on her mind, and her stomach was doing all kinds of crazy cartwheels. She couldn't go through with this. She couldn't. If she was having palpitations already and all they were doing was discussing this, how on earth would she be able to get through the marriage ceremony and live with him?

For a year?

When she barely knew him?

Why had she not considered this properly before?

Because of her mother's phone call earlier, for extra money, for more tests.

That was why.

"I have an answer for you," he said, "I can do this. I want to, if it helps you."

She stared back at him as his words landed in her heart. *If it helps you.*

"Really?"

"If I'm being completely honest, I could do with the extra cash. I presume you can, too, otherwise you wouldn't have come to me." His eyes were warm, and soft, and she found a sense of calm, looking into them. As calm as looking at the sea had been. "You're okay to do this?" she asked, weakly.

"Like you said, we're not killing anyone and we're not doing anything too illegal, although that's debatable. But, for sure, the cats don't need the money as badly as you do."

"Can we go for a walk first?" she suggested, suddenly overcome with the sudden desire to keep moving.

"Sure."

So they walked.

"You seem nervous," he said, guessing her mood.

"I am."

"Second thoughts?"

"Yes." She glanced at him. "You must think I'm insane"

He smiled, and it made her heart dip. Why did it now? Why?

"I've always thought you're slightly, *cutely* insane."

"Cutely insane? Really?"

"Given the last few days, yes." He drew in a breath. "I figure you must need this, otherwise why else would you ask me, of all people?"

She looked away, finding it hard to stare at him when he spoke so candidly.

"I've been thinking," he continued. "I've had all weekend to think about this, and you're right, this is insane. But, we either decide to do this, or forget about it, but since you came to me, I'm willing to help you out."

"Why?" she asked.

"Why?"

She nodded. She needed to know. It was one thing her asking him for a favor, but he didn't know her. Why would he agree? Apart from the money? Though that was a pretty huge incentive.

"Who would say no to half a million dollars?" he looked down at her, and they stopped walking, and now stood face to face.

"You'd have to put up with me for a year," she said, testing him. Saying it out aloud in the bright summer sunlight, with no flickering restaurant candles to hide their deepest fears, made it that much more real.

"I could do that, easily."

"Easily?" she asked, wondering why he thought it would be easy to live with a stranger. With her.

"You'd have to put up me for a year," he challenged.

"It was either you or Rufus Wilson."

"Is he an ex-boyfriend?"

"Goodness, no!" The thought of her work colleague made her screw up her face. She'd caught him picking his nose a few days ago, and had flinched in disgust. "He's a work colleague. The only one who's still single, and I understand why."

"No ex-boyfriends you could have gone to?"

She shook her head. "Ex-boyfriends are better left in the past."

This seemed to satisfy him.

"But," and this was a new revelation, something she hadn't considered. "Are there any girlfriends lurking around, any wanna-be-girlfriends? Because I'd hate to get in the way of anything."

"There's nothing to worry about in that regard."

"Nothing?" She wanted to make sure.

"Well," he put his hands into his pockets, and stared away into the distance, a grin breaking out on his face. "Ralph, my foreman, is always trying to set me up with his niece. Says she's a couple of years younger than me but he's convinced we'd get on like a house on fire."

"And?" she asked, feeling something prickly in her chest. Not jealousy, but something prickly all the same at this.

He stared back at her. "I'm quite capable of finding my own woman."

"And the reason you haven't?" she asked, eager to find out more about him.

"Is because I've been busy building up the business. I haven't had time for romance."

"This would suit us fine," she said, thinking things through from a practical point of view.

"One year? It will fly."

His words seemed to tilt her decision. She could do this,

because Blake seemed confident, albeit more confident than she felt.

Since when had she ever looked to anyone, least of all him, for validation?

"You'll have to live at my apartment, though."

"In your apartment?" he asked.

He looked shocked. You haven't thought about that, have you? The day to day of our lives," she said.

"No." He raked a hand through his hair. "I hadn't thought about it at all."

"You can think about it, for another day or so."

He paused for a moment, then said, "Okay. I've thought about it and I can do it."

She laughed. "I meant think about it properly. I'd feel safer in my own place. It's not ideal, I know."

He nodded. "You can trust me," he said, then laughed. "That's what murderers and kidnappers probably say when they're luring their victim."

"Not a good analogy," she said.

He dipped his head. "Sorry. It's not. But, yeah. I can live at your apartment."

"In case someone from the lawyer's office shows up to do a spot check. I don't know how you'll feel about sleeping on the couch. I only have a small apartment, and there's only one bedroom."

"I can manage the couch."

"For a year?" she asked.

"For the reward, definitely yes."

"And we have our boundaries—"

"I know. You've already told me, Shay."

"Though to outside eyes we need to look like a married couple." The insides of her stomach turned upside down as she tentatively reached out and took his hand. His eyes widened in surprise.

"Just ... " she swallowed. "Just trying you out for size."

His hand didn't go limp, but remained soft. His skin was warm, and because he hadn't made a move, she felt braver, and entwined her fingers in his.

He looked at her. "Okay?"

She nodded.

He didn't do anything; he seemed to be following her lead, taking her direction.

She squeezed his hand gently, and he closed his fingers slightly around hers. "Is that okay?"

She nodded, then exhaled loudly. "Can we do this?" she asked.

"I think we can, but it doesn't matter what I think. What do you think?"

"I think we can," she replied. "And the equation says it makes sense."

"The equation?"

"Marriage plus one year of living with a stranger equals…" The sum of twenty-one million dollars dangled before her. Even though she would never inherit that sum, it was so huge and unbelievable, that he would never believe her, but he didn't need to know that. This was only going to be a one year contract.

"Equals?"

"Happiness," she replied.

He laughed. "What's so funny?" she asked.

"I had a list of weighted pros and cons, and in the end there were more pros than cons."

"We think the same way," he said.

"Yes, we do." It made everything easier, somehow. They were on the same wavelength having approached this logically and rationally. They both squeezed their hands at the same time.

"Will you marry me?" he asked, his face suddenly serious. Then he shrugged, and lowered his voice. "I'm not going to get on my knee, because this isn't the real thing, but ... for authenticity's sake... will you, Shay Donovan, marry me?" Then, "this feels odd," he whispered.

"I know." Though, for a tiny split-second moment, her heart rate sped up. Goosebumps popped up all over her skin.

It's only fake, she told herself, as her pulse galloped at breakneck speed.

"Think of the equation," Blake told her.

She did, then said, "I will marry you." And then, because this was all new, and a part of her was wary and cautious, "No kissing, or funny stuff."

"I won't lay a finger on you, and that's a promise."

"I've got the legal documents to show you, to prove that I'm not playing a bad prank on you." She'd managed to find some paperwork which didn't state the monetary value of the will. Blake took a read through and seemed satisfied.

"We should plan the quickie wedding. I can only take a few days off work. We'll have to go to Las Vegas," she told him.

"Las Vegas?" he asked.

"That's right. We'll need a ID, and a quick trip to the courthouse to get a license, then off to the chapel for a quick five minute wedding, and we need to do it this week"

"So soon?

She reminded him of her aunt's time clause.

"How does this week sound, on Wednesday?" It would give her time to complete outstanding tasks at work. They could go on Wednesday and be back at work by Thursday

"Vegas here we come," he said.

CHAPTER 15

Things were happening at lightning speed.

After the walk along the seafront, they returned to their respective apartments.

Over the next day or so, Blake booked the flight tickets, and made sure to book separate rooms at the hotel while Shay concentrated on the wedding arrangements.

Wedding arrangements.

Every so often he would stop and ponder on this strange new route his life had taken.

As for work, he'd told Ralph and Nancy that he had another business trip to tend to and that he'd be back in a few days.

He could already hear Ralph asking questions.

Shay had told him she'd come up with a similar excuse, though, since she wasn't the boss and didn't own the company, things would be different for her.

He was really doing this. And so was she.

They would soon be husband and wife.

They flew together, meeting at the airport then boarding to the short flight to Las Vegas as strangers, only to return a day later as Mr. and Mrs. Kennedy.

They checked in, and agreed to meet an hour later, to do the deed.

He hadn't even bought a ring. She'd told him not to, and had mentioned that these things could be brought from any of the places along the Vegas Strip. And sure enough, they'd found a place selling dirt cheap wedding bands.

He wasn't sure how to dress up. Whether to be really spruced up. They hadn't discussed clothes.

Why would they?

It wasn't the real thing.

But, an hour later, he was waiting in the lobby of the hotel, dressed in a dark shirt and smart business suit.

"You dressed up?" she asked, sounding somewhat surprised. She wore a simple white summer dress. He sucked in a breath, because he was so used to seeing her in dark business colors, and this was completely unexpected.

She looked heavenly.

Dark hair, dark eyes, no spectacles. Light makeup. And that dress. Soft fabric, strappy, and slightly loose, but accentuating her shapely figure.

Holy smokes.

"You look... you look..." What should he say? Being mindful of their alliance, he couldn't say what he really wanted to; that she looked amazing and she took his breath away.

She wasn't his wife, no more than she was his girlfriend.

Remember the money, he told himself in an effort to steel himself. "You look summery," he said, unable to take his eyes off her.

"You look handsome," she returned, making him feel sheepish that he hadn't paid her the compliment she deserved. She looked away quickly.

"Are you nervous?" he asked, because he could sense an anxiety about her.

"It feels real now."

"If you don't want to go through with this, we don't have to."

"We're here now; we've flown all this way and we can't turn back now."

He touched her arm. "If you're not sure, we can turn back," he said, lowering his voice.

She didn't look like a happy fake bride either. He couldn't do this if she still had regrets, and heck, he was only doing this to help her, and, just as much as for the money. He lowered his voice. "If you're not okay with this, we don't have to go ahead." People were walking past in the busy hotel lobby which was full of couples, and this didn't seem the right conversation to have just before the wedding ceremony. The chapel, she'd informed him, was only two blocks away.

She looked up at him and looked so scared that he placed his fingers gently on her arms, almost as if he was afraid to touch her. "You look as if you're realizing this is a mistake."

She frowned at his words, so he lowered his head and whispered close to her ear. "Say the word and we can stop, Shay."

She pulled away. "We've come all the way here to do this and we're going to do it. I'm having last minute jitters; I'd probably have them even if this was the real thing."

"But it's not the real thing."

She laughed, uneasily. "I know. That's why I should lighten up. We need this, you and I, we could both do with the ...the reward, and I'll feel better once it's done."

He pressed his lips together because he wasn't sure himself. It was one thing to see her every month at the meetings, and there hadn't been more than a passing interest as far as he was concerned but he'd seen her more than a few times in the last few days, in such a short space of time, and he felt that he knew her better now. And because of that he was finding it hard to hide his feelings.

How would he last a year?

He wanted to tell her that a wedding wasn't something that was just 'done', but he didn't know if she would understand what he meant. "If you're sure," he said.

"I'm sure. We'll do the thing, then stay here tonight and fly back tomorrow. We'll be back at work in the afternoon, as planned, and no one will be any wiser. It will be easy."

"Easy?" he asked, because he doubted her words. She was saying the right things, but something had set her on edge. Nerves, perhaps.

"It's easy," she said, in reply to his question. "I'm feeling out of sorts because of the heat."

He looked at her oddly, and she had a feeling he didn't believe her because the lobby of the hotel was air conditioned and there was no heat in here to affect her temperament.

It was only Blake, but she couldn't tell him that.

She wasn't nervous because of the wedding.

She wasn't having doubts.

She wasn't.

She had every intention of going through with this, because her father was sick, and this was her only way to help him. And because, the inheritance would help her, too.

But a peculiar feeling had settled in the pit of her stomach. It was more than nerves. She stared at her reflection in the mirror and felt a sense of sadness. She'd worn her white summer dress; she'd chosen white, because it was the color of a wedding dress, even if the style of dress wasn't, and it was so hot here in Vegas this time of the year. *Too* hot.

But it wasn't a wedding dress, any more than this was a wedding.

Still, she'd made an effort with her hair and makeup, and putting in her contact lenses.

She was still getting married.

Sort of.

But she hadn't been prepared for Blake to show up looking the way he had.

And, goodness, he looked so handsome. She'd only caught a glimpse of him from the side as soon as the elevator doors had opened, but it had almost made her heart stop.

She'd never seen him look all dressed up.

She'd taken a moment to catch her breath before she'd stepped out of the elevator.

He'd made an effort.

Almost as if this was the real thing.

And as she walked towards him, the thought smacked into her: what if this had been the real thing?

What she had only come to realize now was that underneath that rugged exterior lay a caring man. The two or three years of small talk at town hall meetings hadn't given her too deep of an insight into the real man. But everything from the past few weeks, from the Heimlich maneuver to their conversations had shown her another side to him.

One she had not been prepared for.

One she had not expected, because she'd never thought of Blake in that way.

It had always been Rourke who had occupied that crazy fantasy-crush in her heart.

And now they had been thrown together and everything he said or did showed him to be a perfect gentleman. Blake had interpreted her nervousness incorrectly just now.

She wasn't having second doubts about this hare-brained idea for them to marry; she was questioning the way her feelings had changed towards him.

It was the way he had whispered close to her ear; that had started it, that and his concern for her peace of mind. These things had set off a chain reaction inside her that had made her insides turn soft like honey. When he'd placed his hands ever-so-gently on her arms, and moved in closer to whisper, his hot breath had caressed her neck and made her shiver.

So, no. It wasn't doubt that was making her hesitate; it was that she was now questioning her changing feelings towards this man.

Confusion swirled around her and muddied her thoughts.

If she felt weird now after a plane ride from Starling Bay to Vegas, what would it feel like after a year of living with him and pretending to be his wife?

"Let's go and get married," she said, and, needing to prove to herself that he wasn't having an effect on her, she slipped her hand into his, and they walked out of the hotel.

The walk was short, since the wedding chapel was close by.

The room was hot and stuffy, and she was in a daze as they walked in. She'd barely had time to center herself, when the Elvis lookalike who had conducted the ceremony, said, "You may now kiss the bride." She looked at Blake, stared at his face, at his strong jaw and his eyes. Her heartbeat was racing so fast she thought her heart was going to explode.

She expected Blake to move closer, to lower his head and to pull her towards him, and she waited for these things to happen, but instead he lifted her hand and brought it to his lips, then dropped a chaste kiss on it.

The pastor laughed. "Is that the best you can manage? You're marrying her, not buying her at an auction."

They both turned and looked at him in surprise. Then they looked at one another. Their gazes locked and held there for a heartbeat. His eyes were soft, yet still he made no move. It was as if he didn't want to step out of his boundaries; she'd laid them out so clearly and so many times during the past few days: no kissing, no sleeping in the same bed, no hugging, no physical contact, and he didn't seem to want to change them.

She felt as if she'd scared him off and since she had set these boundaries, it was up to her to muddy them a little for now, to seal the deal.

Lifting up on her tiptoes, she brushed her lips against Blake's, at the same time inhaling his refreshing pine and minty scent.

It was like a loaded Cupid's arrow to her chest.

She was suddenly swept away by a whirlwind of emotion.

"Congratulations, you are now Mr. and Mrs. Kennedy!" Elvis cried.

The witness clapped, and brought her out of her dreamlike bubble.

They turned to walk away, and then she remembered: the marriage certificate.

She grabbed it, and then they left.

CHAPTER 16

Shay had kissed him.

And he was now married to her.

If it was weird for him—even knowing that it wasn't real—how much weirder was it for Shay?

Weddings, and everything about them, from the dresses to the menu, were a big deal for women. He knew this from his sister. Weddings were huge.

He looked at Shay to try to gauge how she felt, but she was looking straight ahead.

As they left the chapel and stepped back onto the dry heat of a noon-sun, the people bustling passed them and bumping into them made him want to step away into the quiet somewhere and take a moment.

Shay was quiet, and he let her be. It wasn't until they were more than a few hundred yards away that he realized they were holding hands. In fact, Shay was gripping his hand tightly; not too tight so it was hurting him but tight enough that he could feel the pressure of her slim fingers against his.

He didn't say anything but he could sense she was wrapped up in her own world and she needed to be with her own thoughts; so he didn't say a word. He was curious to know what was going on inside her head, but he also didn't want to pry. But when she speeded up, he was forced to ask her. "Where are you going?"

She seemed in a hurry.

"I was heading back to our hotel." She stopped for a moment on the busy sidewalk.

He opened his mouth, and then closed it, not wanting to show his surprise.

So soon?

They had the day ahead of them.

He'd been thinking that maybe they'd go somewhere and talk, even have a drink. A real drink to toast the unreal wedding.

"We should go for a drink to mark the occasion," he said.

"A drink?" She didn't look keen.

"I know it's not real, Shay, but my throat is parched."

"Okay." She shrugged, the shrug telling him that this was the last thing on her mind, but he wasn't ready to go back and sit in his hotel room all by himself just yet.

This event had to be celebrated, or highlighted by *something.*

So, they walked into the next bar they found, and were soon sitting across the table from one another. He had a bottle of beer, she had ordered homemade lemonade.

He raised his glass. "To us," he said.

"To us."

He took a long swig of his beer, and relaxed, and it wasn't until then that he realized how uptight and strained all the muscles in his body had been.

"You okay?" he asked, seeing that Shay didn't seem relaxed at all. Her demeanor reminded him of her financial woes, and he assumed that that was why she was down. And because this lie, the one they had created, was so big.

Shay had never seemed to him like a big risk-taker. In all his dealings with her, in all their conversations, she seemed to be sensible and practical. Doing something like this was not what he expected from her.

He guessed she was in big trouble, or, maybe she also wanted an easier life. If he stood to gain half a million dollars, how much did she stand to inherit?

Had she split the money, or did she stand to inherit more? His friend Reed was seeing a friend of Shay's. Maybe Shay had seen what money could bring; maybe it was as simple as that?

This new life that they were going to live for the next year was potentially going to be difficult for them both. Maybe difficult was the wrong word—for they had gotten on fine, the entire trip here and checking into their hotel—everything was as fine and as normal as it could have been given the circumstances.

But the next year could be a testing time.

He didn't really know her and she didn't know him and therefore, despite having spent the last week talking about their new life and getting to know one another, they were still relative strangers who were only coming together for one purpose.

Money.

But he worked at the factory and he would still spend long hours there. He wouldn't always be at her apartment, and he could eat out most of the time if he wanted. He usually had takeouts at work.

Nothing new there.

They could get through this year by staying out of one another's way.

The only problem in all this would be him having to sleep on a couch for a year. He'd have to wait and see how that worked out.

And if things got too much he could always go back to his place if he needed some alone time.

They drank quietly. He'd hoped they might talk and get back

some of that easy familiarity that they'd had on the plane ride to Vegas, but she seemed more distant now that they were married.

"Would you mind if I went back to the hotel?" she asked suddenly.

"Don't you want to finish your drink?"

"I'm not that thirsty."

"I'll come with you," he said.

"You don't have to go back because of me. You could explore the city. It's getting too hot for me. I think I need to lie down."

"I'll head back, too and get a nap. I'm tired from the plane ride."

"Are you sure you're going to be okay?" he asked again, when they returned to the hotel. They walked along the corridor to their rooms. Hers was directly opposite his.

"I need to rest up for a while and check up on some work things on my phone."

Clearly, she needed her space. It wasn't an ideal way to spend a wedding night, and while he knew this wasn't an ideal wedding, he had been hoping that they would at least have dinner together later on.

CHAPTER 17

She returned to her hotel room because her mother had texted her twice while she was at the bar with Blake. It was nothing to worry about, her mother texted, and she knew that because they were only texts, it wasn't too urgent. Her mother would have called her.

It was simply an update on her father who had gone in for some more tests. As if the marriage lies weren't bad enough, having her mom text her reminded her of why she was doing this, and worry over her father's health had dampened the mood even more.

Add to that, she'd had mixed feelings after she'd kissed Blake and when they'd left the chapel she'd been trying to figure out what her feelings were.

But her mother's call had taken her mind off the marriage ceremony, yet the deception and the fact that she was now Mrs. Blake Kennedy weighed on her, as did the fact that her parents didn't know a thing.

Lies and deceit.

These things didn't sit well with her.

She didn't even want to think about how much more

complicated things would be once Blake moved in with her. This was something they had planned for him to do the following weekend.

Maybe things wouldn't be as bad as she was worried they might be. After all, being with him on the trip here hadn't been as awkward as she had feared. Even the wedding ceremony hadn't been too bad, once she'd calmed down a little and walked into the chapel with him.

But, for a brief moment the thought flitted across her mind that she had only ever wanted to walk up the aisle once; and she'd never in her wildest dreams imagined that it would be in a cheap tacky little wedding Chapel in Las Vegas.

Blake, dressed the way he had been, had made her heart jolt. She and Jenna had often discussed romantic feelings and guys and dating, and the notion that having an attraction to someone somehow made that person seem more attractive in your eyes.

She was finding this to be the case with Blake now.

Walking along the strip, sitting with him in the bar, trying to come to grips with the idea that he was her husband, all of it was still new and having an effect on her. She could tell he didn't want to go back to the hotel that he could have happily had another drink, but her mother's texts had left her feeling unsettled.

She returned to her room and called her mom.

"Hi, mom. How's dad?"

"He's okay, sweetie."

But she could sense the worry in her mother's voice.

"What is it, mom?"

"Nothing, sweetie."

"You said he had some more tests."

"He did."

"And?"

Her mom didn't say anything.

"Mom? What about the tests." Her breath caught in her throat.

"I don't want to worry you, sweetie. Not while you're on your course." She'd lied and told her mother that she was away on a short course.

"I'll worry more if you don't tell me, Mom.

"They found a shadow on your father's other lung."

Shadow on his other lung.

Shay's body slouched into itself.

Please, god. Don't let this be *that* thing.

Let his healthy lung stay healthy.

"What did they say?"

"They need to do a CT scan, and they'll be able to tell us more."

"What does dad say?"

"He wanted to know when you'd be over next."

"I'll come as soon as I get back, Mom. Tell him that for me."

"I will, sweetie. I have to go, the doctor wants to speak to me."

"Love you, Mom. Tell dad I love him, too."

She hung up feeling a blanket of dread swallowing her up. This wasn't the news she'd been expecting. Her father had seemed to respond well to the chemo, and the last thing he needed was something else like this to strike him down again.

She spent the next few hours crying, and feeling in the depths of despair, and then she fell asleep.

When Blake called her a few hours later, to ask if she wanted to get anything to eat, she declined, citing a headache. She could hear the disappointment in his voice, but she wasn't up to eating dinner.

But then she felt guilty.

He'd come all this way, and had gone along with this ruse because he wanted to help her.

Poor man.

Poor man who stood to make half a million dollars.

But, he had gotten married for her sake.

It seemed unfair to stay in her room and leave him alone, and she would only get more depressed staring at the four walls and thinking of her dad.

So, she changed her mind, and told him that she'd meet him in the hotel lobby at eight.

She had agreed to meet him for dinner and that in itself had lifted his spirits. He'd booked into one of the more upscale restaurants at the Bellagio, and if at first Shay had seemed a little down when he saw her, as soon as they walked into the restaurant, her sprits lifted.

"I've only ever seen this in films," she said, "And even then from the outside."

"Happy?" he asked, feeling good about putting a smile on her face.

"Yes," she nodded.

They were seated, and ordered a feast, and this evening seemed not so different from the dinner at The Olive Tree, the night when she'd told him about her Great Aunt Dena and the inheritance.

The night that had led to this.

"I'm sorry if I was bad company earlier," she said, when they had finished eating.

"A penny for your thoughts?"

"It's nothing."

"Then surely you can share that with me?"

The corners of her lips lifted as she forced a smile. "It's really not something I want to talk about."

"Then let's find something that you do want to talk about."

"I have questions," she said, suddenly looking a little brighter. "Questions I should have asked you before we got married."

This was interesting. His curiosity peaked. "Ask away."

"They're personal questions."

"Ask away."

"You don't mind?" she asked.

"We're married now, and no, I don't."

"Your last girlfriend. How long ago?"

He'd often wondered if she'd ever ask him that question. He was as curious about her past love life, but he was careful not to overstep the mark and decided he wasn't going to pry. "Been over a year."

"How long did you date for?"

"Less than a year."

"And the reason you split up?"

"Didn't spend much time together and she was away a lot, due to the nature of her work."

"Do you still keep in touch?"

"Heck, no. Haven't heard from her since she left town."

"She's not in Starling Bay anymore?"

"Not as far as I know," he replied, and noted the look of relief on her face. "Anything else," he asked when she stopped firing questions at him like rounds of ammunition.

"Any criminal record? Anything I should know about?"

"It's a bit too late to be asking those questions," he said, with a grin.

"We could get the marriage annulled, depending on what you say."

That made him laugh. "You realize we could still get the marriage annulled?"

"I'm not sure how that would work regarding the will. I'd have to ask Frank Barclay."

"Who's he?"

"The lawyer who changed my life…I think…it remains to be seen." She took a sip of her water. "You've never asked me how much I stand to inherit."

He lifted his beer bottle. "That's your business."

"Even after all this, you still don't want to know?" she asked."

"No. It's up to you if you want to tell me."

He noted that she didn't say another word.

"When do you want me to move in?" he asked.

"How about on Saturday?" she suggested.

"Saturday? Are you sure?"

"You're going to have to do it at some time, better to do it sooner rather than later. I'll be scanning copies of the marriage certificate and sending that over to the lawyer as soon as I get back home tomorrow."

"Saturday, then," he said.

"But come over on Friday evening and get a feel for the size of my apartment. It's tiny."

"As long as I have a couch, I'll be fine."

Come what may, he'd made his bed, and he'd have to lie in it now and see this thing through. A year from now, he'd be so much richer.

CHAPTER 18

"Tell him I'll come and see him soon Mom," she said, balancing the phone on her shoulder as she unlocked the door to her apartment having just arrived back from the airport.

"How soon, sweetie?

"At the weekend, Mom."

"I wouldn't ask but this shadow on his lung has really scared your father. He seems to think he won't make it, that he doesn't have long."

Shay put her hand to her mouth. "Don't say that, Mom.

"I'm not saying that, your father is."

"I'll come and see him tonight."

"Tonight?"

"I'll come tonight. I promise." She was already exhausted from these last two days, and now she'd have to freshen up then head back to work. It was a tight call, but her father wanted to see her, and she had no choice.

"That's great, sweetie. I know this will cheer him up."

Shay smiled to herself. "Tell him I'm coming."

Walking through the door, Shay set down her luggage and

closed the door behind her. Her eyes swept over the apartment. It still looked the same. Everything was still the same; there was no reason it wouldn't be, and yet she felt different.

Even though she'd down played this entire marriage event, coming back home today, after a whirlwind two days with Blake made things seem odder than when she had been in Vegas at the wedding chapel.

The normality of her old life contrasted against the craziness of the last few days as she tried to brace herself for what her new life would be like. Outwardly things would be the same, but behind closed doors, with Blake living here, things would be a lot different.

Pushing recent events to the back of her mind, she got changed into her work clothes and was back at work by noon, which was the time she'd told Francine she would be back by.

She'd lied and told her that she'd had to make a quick emergency trip to visit her parents and to see how her dad was.

The real test would begin now; trying to be normal and hide the deception around work and friends.

"You're back," said Francine, hovering around her desk a mere five minutes after she'd sat down at her desk.

"Yes," Shay replied.

"How's your dad?"

"They found a shadow on his other lung," said Shay. Guilt washed over her. How strange that this was the truth, when she had lied and told Francine that her father wasn't well and she was taking time off to go and see him. Funny how life worked out and how it had now dealt a real shock for her.

Francine clasped a hand to her chest. "Sometimes these things turn out to be benign."

"They're going to do some tests and we'll have to wait for the results."

"I'm praying for him," said Francine.

Now she felt even worse. "Thanks."

She pushed her glasses up, and Francine looked at her oddly, then her mouth fell open.

"What's that on your finger? A wedding ring?"

Shay laughed as if this was the craziest thing she'd heard. She'd forgotten to remove her wedding band, and she needed to call Blake and tell him. "Oh, this?" She pulled it off and held it between her fingers. "No, no, no, no." She laughed again, only Francine continued to look at her. "It looks like a wedding band, and you never wear rings." Francine spluttered. "Did you run off and get a quickie wedding, or something?"

Shay almost choked in indignation. "Me? Get married? Do you think I'd get married and not invite you?" She shook her head, "I was trying on some of my mom's costume jewellery, you know, trying to tidy up my mom's drawer and going through her things, trying to pamper her and give her some me-time. It's been really hard on her, what with my dad and all."

Francine's expression turned serious. "I can't begin to imagine, but that doesn't look like costume jewelry. It's not blingy enough."

"Well, it is," Shay insisted. "The boxes were in a mess, so I tidied them up, and then I tried on a couple of my mom's rings just for a laugh."

She stopped, and she wondered if she'd over explained, or talked for too long.

Francine nodded as if she completely understood. "It was nice of you to do that, and to go and see them at a moment's notice. You're a good daughter, Shay. Get settled in and then we need to look over some new hiring requests from a couple of firms. The paperwork arrived while you were away."

"Will do."

She sank into her chair and watched Francine return to her office, then she put the wedding band into her purse and felt proud of herself for thinking on her feet, even though Francine hadn't seemed completely convinced.

But how many white lies had she told in the space of the last ten minutes?

It had been different when it had been only her and Blake. They were both in on the lie together, but this, coming back to work; this was the beginning.

Things weren't going to get any easier. She was bound to let something slip, especially when she visited her parents as she did every week. What were the chances of something slipping?

She picked up the phone to remind Blake to take off his wedding band.

He put on a lumberjack shirt over his T-shirt and left the buttons open, as was his usual style, and got ready to return to work.

But, if he was being one hundred per cent honest with himself, having the one and a half days with Shay in Vegas, dressing up, just a little because he wanted to make an effort for the ceremony had been nice. Spending time with her had been nice. Clearly, he was a workaholic, and Ralph's advice to take time out had proved insightful. Only, he'd never really taken Ralph's advice much; there was always too much to do.

Blake ran his hands through his hair and caught sight of his wedding band. That would have to come off.

He stared at his hand, and pulled his wedding band off, then examined it closely.

This little piece of cheap metal should have carried a lot of meaning but to him it represented lies.

One year.

That was how long he had to lie for, to put up with the charade, to deceive his family and friends.

It wasn't going to be easy. It had seemed easy when he'd flown out. There had been something about spending time with the woman he had admired from a distance, being close to her, talking to her, and sensing her fear and hesitation—all of these things had made an impression on him. He'd wanted to make her happy each moment he was with her, but he noticed she was worried about something for most of the time, and he couldn't do a thing about it.

Shay was everything he had imagined her to be—not only funny and nice and gorgeous but good company, and easy to be around.

There was no drama surrounding her.

They liked the same type of food, and shared the same type of humor, liked the same type of films. They'd had their meals together, had managed to put up with one another through two plane trips, and not had any arguments or disagreements.

He had been prepared for things about her to irritate him and possibly things about him to imitate her but not once did they have a disagreement, not once did they not get on. Or this could be the early honeymoon period when they were on their best behavior and everything was new, and this ruse was a novelty.

It was hard to tell. The real test would be to see if they made it through to the end of the year but so far, it hadn't been bad for two people who only talked once a month. However, the plane ride back home had been less chatty than the trip to Las Vegas.

He decided to head back into work and prepared himself for Ralph's many questions.

"When did you get back?" Ralph asked, sticking his head around the door to his office not long after Blake had walked into his office.

Blake exhaled slowly.

This was the problem with having a husband and wife team working for him; nothing was a secret. Especially when one was his office manager and PA, and the other was his foreman. He was sure Nancy had told him that he was back.

"How did the meeting go?"

Blake cleared his throat. "It went well."

"Where did you go?"

More questions. He expected nothing less from Ralph. He clasped his hands together and felt his jaw tighten.

"Why do you need to know everything?"

Ralphs face stared at him sheepishly. "No particular reason. Nancy says there was nothing in your diary."

Blake ran his hands through his hair in an effort to expel the tension that was in his neck and shoulders. It made things difficult in situations like this.

"I was checking out a new supplier."

"Oh," said Ralph, looking interested. "Who?"

Exasperated, he threw back, "Why do you need to know everything?" in a tone that had a hard edge to it. Ralph looked understandably put out.

"It's just that you've always told me about these things in the past." He shuffled back a few steps, as if he could feel the hostility rolling off Blake in waves.

Blake hadn't intended to speak so brusquely. He now wished that he'd said it was a personal matter, only then he'd probably have another dozen questions to field from Ralph.

Instead, needing Ralph to leave so that he could get back to settling in at work, he replied, "I've had a hard few days. Do you mind? I need to get back to work." Then his cell phone went off. A quick glance told him that it was Shay at the other end.

"I can see you're busy." Ralph looked hurt, and now Blake felt stupid. "I'll let you get back to things." He walked out.

Blake answered the call.

"Hi."

The sound of Shay's voice lifted the tension from his shoulders. "Hey."

"Did you remember to take off your wedding band?" she asked.

"I did. Why?"

"I forgot, and Francine noticed.

"Ooops. What did she say?"

"She joked about me getting married on the sly."

"No way."

"Yes, way."

He laughed, but she didn't join in. "You didn't find it funny?"

"I was scrambling to find a believable explanation."

"And?"

"And I told her I went to see my mom and dad and I was going through my mom's jewelry boxes."

"Nice save."

"You have no idea. That's why I called, to warn you."

"Thanks for the advice, but I took mine off at home. I hate to think what Ralph might have made of it if I hadn't. He already thinks I'm up to something."

"Oh?"

"Long story, I'll explain tomorrow."

"I look forward to hearing all about it."

CHAPTER 19

She'd completely forgotten to go and see her parents.

Going to work after the flight back from Vegas had left her exhausted, both mentally and physically, and she couldn't have done the car trip even if she'd remembered.

However, the next day at work she was finally getting back to normal.

Everything was normal, apart from the few times during the day that she suddenly remembered that she was married.

And she found herself looking around, when she left her office, or her apartment and was outside, looking to see someone she didn't recognize or know, looking out for her.

It was as creepy, as it was weird, but weird had just become a new metaphor for her life.

So, she drove over to see her parents after work.

There were shadows under her mom's eyes and her face was lined heavy with wrinkles. Shay hugged her tightly. "How is he?" she asked.

"Come and see." Her mom led the way. Shay could see her dad resting on the couch. He was a pale shadow of his former self. His hair had thinned, and he looked like a quarter of the man he used to be, withered, and shriveled. That's what chemo did. The chemo that killed the cancer cells and gave him a chance at life. Ironic that it almost killed him in the process.

But he would live.

She was determined that he would get the best care that money could buy, only it was annoying that she couldn't get her hands on the inheritance for a year. Until then, she would have to take out a bigger loan.

"Dad," she said, softly, and then knelt on the floor, beside the couch. "Is he asleep?" she asked her mom.

"He had a nap. He dozes off from time to time. Tell him you're here. Wake him, so we can all try and eat together."

"Dad," she said, tapping her fingers gently on his arm. He opened his eyes slowly. "Shay," he whispered, his lips forming a smile.

"Sorry I didn't come yesterday. I fell asleep."

"You're here now."

She smiled, and held his hand. "Are you ready to eat? Mom says she made dinner. We can eat together tonight."

"Staying?" he asked.

She'd forgotten to bring her overnight bag, but she had clothes here. "Only if you want me to."

"Stay."

"Okay. I'll stay."

They ate, and she watched as her dad fed himself slowly. He was just so bone tired, and everything he did seemed like an effort.

Ralph was avoiding him. Usually, the burly foreman would come into Blake's office at least once a day.

Today? Not once.

Blake ventured out onto the factory floor, and saw him. "I'm sorry for being so sharp with you yesterday," he said, getting straight to the point. Ralph eyed him suspiciously for a moment.

"I was only asking. I always ask, that's all," said Ralph. "Everything okay?"

Blake considered the question. "Yeah." Because things were good. He was going to Shay's apartment tonight—his home for the next year, and for a reason he didn't understand fully, he was looking forward to it.

"Because, you know, if there's anything you want to talk about, you know where I am."

"I know, Ralph. I know."

"You're leaving early?"

"Yeah, why?"

"It's just that you never do," countered Ralph.

"I have plans." He had plans to go home and shower, and then make his way over to Shay's. Ralph's eyebrows lifted in that way when he knew he was onto something, and Blake almost regretted seeking him out in order to apologize.

"Is this anything to do with your *supplier* meeting the other day?"

"What are you? Sherlock Holmes?"

Ralph grinned. "So, it *is* something to do with that? Must have been one heck of a supplier."

Blake turned around to leave, lifting his arms in the air in a dismissive gesture. "I only came here to apologize, Ralph."

He had important things to consider. Shay had told him to bring a few toiletries and maybe some clothes, so that he could see how much space she had and to move some things over.

He had those kinds of issues to be dealing with, not pandering to Ralph's nosey questions.

Around eight o'clock, he parked up outside her apartment, but when he knocked on her door, with a small suitcase full of his belongings, nobody answered. He didn't think anything of it, but instead surveyed the area around. It was a quiet enough street.

He waited, and then rang the doorbell again.

And when she still didn't answer, he started to get irritated. The longer he waited, the more irritated he became. After a few more moments, it was evident that Shay wasn't there, so he returned to his car and called her.

Her dad had gone to sleep, and Shay was in the kitchen talking to her mom.

"How was your course, sweetie?" her mom asked as Shay wiped down the countertops, and her mother put away the dishes from the dishwasher.

"It was alright."

"It's nice that they're sending you on these things. I suppose you need more training, what with the promotion?"

Shay gulped because she hated lying. "Yeah." She wiped the countertop a little more vigorously than was needed.

"So, how was it? Did they put you up in a nice hotel?"

"Uh… it was okay.

"Okay?"

"Mom," she turned around, trying not to sound irritated. "It was. It was all okay. It was only for one night."

"I'm only asking because it's something new to talk about; something that has nothing to do with your father's cancer." Her mother's lower lip trembled, "All day, that's all I hear, that's the only news, the only thing to talk about."

Shay put down her cloth, walked over to her mother and gave her a hug. "I'm sorry." If things were hard for her father she imagined they were as hard on her mother, being the caregiver, and being the support person for him, while having no one to help her, having no one ask her how she was doing.

"You have a nice boss."

"Francine is good to me. Now, why don't you go and watch TV, and take it easy, Mom," she suggested. "Let me finish off in here. I'll get up if dad needs anything during the night."

Her mother laughed. "He won't bother you. It's me he'll want at his beck and call. I don't mean that in a nasty way, but he will."

"Then I'll make breakfast tomorrow, and tidy the house as best as I can. You can sleep in late tomorrow morning."

"I don't want to sleep in. I can't lie in bed and not think about everything. I worry, about your dad, and the healthcare costs and all sorts of things."

"I told you, Mom. You don't have to worry about that. The promotion has been great, and I get…I get a bigger commission for all the people I place. And business is great. We're so busy, you wouldn't believe it."

"I hate that you're splitting yourself in two places, working so hard and coming to see us and helping out here."

"What else can I do, Mom? I want to help out wherever I can." She turned her back to her mother and re-wiped the surface.

"Francine obviously thinks you're doing a great job."

She stopped for a moment and rubbed her brow, feeling suddenly swept up in the swirl of lies and deceit. After the two days in Vegas, and the wedding, and lying to Francine, and now lying to her mom, she was seriously beginning to wonder if she would ever be able to keep this up for more than a few weeks.

"We don't know what we'd do without you, sweetie."

Shay stared at the patterned tiles on the wall, not wanting to face her mother, but she turned around and forced the smile. "I've had the best parents." She ground down on her teeth and reminded herself that this time next year, all of this would be forgotten. Her dad would get well, and she would have paid off her loans and debts, and she and Blake would go their separate ways.

Just then her phone rang, interrupting her thoughts and she quickly took off her cleaning gloves to answer it. Her heart tripped a beat as soon as she heard Blake's voice.

"Where are you?" he asked.

"Oh…I'm…" she paused, feeling oddly short of breath.

"I'm outside your apartment."

"Where?" She sucked in a breath.

She'd forgotten.

Blake was coming over tonight to scope out her apartment. And he was there now. With his belongings. "I'm so sorry, I've completely forgotten."

Her mom looked at her, curiously. Shay turned her back and stared out of the window.

"Will you be long?" Blake asked.

She bit her lip. "I'm staying at my parents' house tonight."

"You are?"

"I'm really sorry."

"Okay," he laughed. "I suppose it's easy to forget that you have a husband now."

She squeezed her eyes shut and prayed that her mother hadn't heard anything, and to avoid further problems, she walked out of the kitchen. "My mom asked me to stay over. I needed to see my parents."

"You don't have to explain, Shay. It's a simple enough mistake to make."

"Did I mess up your plans?"

"I didn't really have any plans, except to come over to your apartment tonight. Or maybe I should say *our* apartment?"

She heard him chuckle, but with her mother's ears probably straining to hear, she was in no mood for humor. "I'll be back tomorrow."

"Tomorrow, then."

"Okay."

"Do you want me to actually move in tomorrow?"

She glanced over her shoulder. It was too much to think about right now, but they had decided this already. "Let's stick to the plan." She lowered her voice. "Bring your things."

"I shall bring my things," he said, mimicking her.

"I can't really talk properly," she explained.

"I can tell."

"Sorry."

"Stop apologizing, Shay."

"Tomorrow, then."

"Tomorrow."

She walked back into the living room to find her mom on the couch, with the TV on. "Who was that?" her mom asked, matter-of-factly.

"It was a friend."

"Francine?" She was sure her mother had heard something. Or the male sounding voice on the other end.

"No," then, to change the subject, and because she was curious, she said, "Mom, tell me about Great Aunt Dena."

Her mother's eyes opened wider. "Great Aunt Dena?"

Shay shrugged. "That's an unusual name, for starters. I'd have expected her to be a Charlotte, or an Emily."

Her mother looked at her in amazement. "I don't know why they called her Dena. Your grandmother said that Dena's parents traveled a lot. They were creative, literary people. Who knows? But why on earth do you want to know about her?"

Shay wondered if her mom knew that she had passed away. "I'm curious, that's all. Did you ever meet her?"

"Goodness, no! She kept herself to herself. Why do you ask?"

"You've never heard from her?"

Her mother shook her head.

"Is she still alive?" Shay asked, testing her mom.

"I should think not. She was old. I think she died a long time ago."

Shay sat back and chewed on her mom's words and how much she didn't know. And how one day she would tell her mom about her Great Aunt Dena.

CHAPTER 20

*H*e had packed a small suitcase. *Tiny.*

So worried was he of imposing on Shay. He shouldn't have felt that way, but he did.

The truth was, he wasn't sure exactly how to feel about any of this, and he was certain that she was as lost as he was, even though on the surface of it all, they both seemed to be fine.

It wasn't fine.

It couldn't be.

They 'd just make a huge move, and this secondary one—for him to move in with her—was as big, if not bigger than the decision to have the fake marriage.

Living together?

In name only, and as friends.

Given the fact that he was a man and he already felt odd, he wondered how Shay felt now that the reality of their situation was sinking in.

Sometime during the late afternoon the next day, he returned to Shay's apartment, and rang the doorbell.

"Don't be alarmed," he said, when Shay opened the door and stared at his luggage. She had impressed upon him that her apartment was tiny, and he had made sure not to bring too much with him. "It might look like a lot, but it's not. I don't envisage there being too many clothes because I can bring this suitcase back and forth instead of—"

"Don't worry about it. There's no need to over explain, and no need to do what you just said."

"Did I say too much?"

She nodded. "Are you nervous?"

"The truth?" he asked, glad that she'd picked up on his mood. "Yes. A little."

"Good, because that makes two of us. Come in."

So he did.

"Let me give you a grand tour of my palace," she said in a posh voice, then added, with a grin, "It will take all of twenty seconds." She showed him around her place. It was small, but he had been prepared. She waved her hand to the side. "That's the kitchen," then she waved another hand to the room they were in. "This is the living room. Follow me." She flung open the door to her bedroom. "My room, and opposite," she walked out and opened the door opposite. "This is the bathroom. I've cleared some space for you on the shelves." She pointed to a small shelf.

"Thanks. Very considerate of you."

"And this," she said, walking back into her living room, "is for your clothes." She showed him a small chest of drawers which looked out of place in the already tiny living room. "I cleared this out for you and moved it here. I figured it made sense for it to be here and not in my bedroom since you'll be sleeping here." She made an apologetic face.

"That's great, thanks." Maybe because he'd been hyped up and had expected everything to be super tiny, he was suitably prepared, and in the end, it wasn't as bad as he had imagined it to be.

He had room to put his things, and this chest of drawers was more than he'd hoped for.

"We're really doing this," he said, as he took his clothes out of his suitcase and started to place them into the chest of drawers

"You can't back out now, we're married."

He grinned.

She rested her back against the wall, so she could see his face.

"What's so funny?" she asked.

"You have to laugh; otherwise it will be much harder to get through this."

Laughter made things lighter, took the tension out of awkward situations, such as this one. He'd felt awkward when she'd showed him the bathroom. Two weeks ago he'd barely known Shay, and only as a person he met at the town hall every month. And now he would be living in her apartment, showering in her shower, eating and sleeping here.

"Do you find this difficult?" he asked, closing the drawers. His suitcase was empty save for the toiletries which he had yet to place in the bathroom.

"Difficult? My friend Jenna stayed here for a few months. It's not difficult, we simply have to get used to one another. Obviously, this will be different, because Jenna's my friend, and you're…" She didn't finish the sentence.

"I understand," he said, standing up. "It's going to take some getting used to." He moved his suitcase to the side and out of the way. Now it was just him and her.

He cast his eye over the room.

There was no question about it; they were going to be in one another's faces.

"We should say things as they are," he said, advocating total honesty. "And always tell the truth."

"The truth," she said, agreeing. "No secrets."

"No secrets," he replied.

"Can I get you a cold drink or something?" she asked, pushing off from the wall.

He was eager to oblige. Anything that would put her at ease. "Something cold would be good."

～

How was this going to work?

Her heartbeat was exploding, like firecrackers on a fourth of July parade.

It was one thing being with Blake Kennedy at a hotel, or walking down the street with him in Vegas, but having him be here, inside her crowded little apartment was something else altogether. She felt funny pouring out the iced tea for them both into glasses, sensing that he was watching her.

Could he tell she was nervous?

And how was this going to work? She was getting palpitations thinking about them sleeping with only a few walls separating them.

And the shower

Not to mention the use of the toilet.

She wiped her brow, feeling hot all of a sudden because she hadn't properly considered any of this.

"Shay?"

He stood behind her. She inhaled deeply, counted to three, and turned around. "Here you go," she said, passing him the glass of iced tea.

There was no table here in the tiny kitchen, although there was one in the living room, but she preferred standing, in this situation, and she made no move to go over the living room.

"Cheers," he said, lifting his glass.

He looked at ease, and completely unruffled, as if this was a piece of cake for him.

"Cheers," she said, if a little weakly, because her voice had suddenly lost its loudness.

Why had she never noticed how tall and slim he was?

She'd been rooted to the spot when she'd opened the door to him earlier and seen him in a T-shirt and jeans. He'd been dressed casually, without his signature lumberjack shirt and now she was able to clearly see his muscles. He'd looked like someone who had walked off a photo shoot for sexy male calendars.

Had she really not noticed him before?

Had Rourke Halloran really taken up all of her powers of attention?

She'd backed away from the door, motioned him to come in and was thankful that she hadn't knocked anything over as she'd shown him around her apartment, for all of the two seconds that it took.

And then she'd admired his back view, as he placed his toiletries in her bathroom, and later, she'd watched as he put away his clothes in the chest of drawers she had hastily cleared for him.

It was intimate, and weird him being here; it made her feel ditzy, as if she wasn't sure how to behave around him. And she was worried that she would never sleep another wink at night again.

Now he was standing in her kitchen, drinking her iced tea, in her glass, looking at her with those mesmerising gray eyes.

She took a sip of her iced tea, and then placed her hand back on the countertop behind her, hoping to strike a nonchalant pose, but instead she knocked over the empty iced tea cans, which she then bent down to retrieve.

"How are we going to handle the cooking, and cleaning, and groceries?" he asked.

"We'll have to play it by ear. This is a first time for me as well." She couldn't look at him for too long because it did strange things to her insides. Things she'd never noticed before.

Now, it was too much. Too intense. Too sultry. Too sexy.

Maybe she was coming down with something? It wasn't inconceivable. After all, she'd left her parents' house in the early afternoon, after convincing her mom to go for a walk and to get some fresh air. She'd done her best to tidy up the house and to make lunch, helping her mom in any way she could, and then she'd spent time with her dad. When she arrived back at her apartment, she already felt as if she'd done enough for the entire weekend, but she'd had to clear out her chest of drawers and drag it all the way into the living room.

This, with Blake in her apartment, was turning out to be more tiring and emotionally more difficult than the morning she'd spent at her parent's place.

"How about we get a takeout this evening?" she asked, in an attempt to talk about something easy.

"Sounds good."

"Pizza?"

"I'll eat anything. I don't mind. What would you prefer?" he asked.

"Pizza is good. Shall I order it now or later?"

"I'm easy. Up to you."

"Later."

She couldn't eat now even if she was starving. The thought of sitting in her living room, with Blake, eating dinner, and then what?

Watching TV?

Talking?

And sleeping.

What if she wanted to watch TV and he wanted to go to sleep?

How would that work?

The solution was to buy another TV for her bedroom. Or move the existing one into her bedroom, but what if Blake wanted to watch TV?

"Are you overthinking things, Shay?" he asked. The fact that he had so accurately read her mind freaked her out. She let out a false little laugh. "No."

The way he looked at her told her he didn't really believe her.

Then he went on to ask her about her parents, and where they lived and whether she had any siblings. She told him that she sometimes stayed there, and that they were an hour's drive in the next town, but she didn't mention her father's illness. She discovered that he had a sister who was married and lived in Canada, and his parents lived in California.

They'd done it all back to front; gotten married first and then started to get to know one another better. They continued to talk still standing up in the kitchen, and even if it felt slightly odd to be doing this, neither of them suggested moving to the living room in order to get more comfortable.

Then they went on to talk about their return to work after Vegas. She told him about Francine noticing her ring and how she had managed to get out of that.

He told her about his suspicious foreman.

She told him that she had sent a copy of the marriage certificate to the lawyer and that he had called to congratulate on her on the marriage.

"He congratulated you?"

She nodded. "So now he knows."

"And did he say anything about the spot checks? When or how often?"

"That would defeat the objective."

He nodded in agreement. "It would indeed. I guess this means we have to always be acting like a married couple."

"Whatever that means," she threw back.

"I guess it means holding hands when we're out, and doing things that couples do."

"Not all things," she pointed out.

"Not those things, no." His words made her blush. "I meant like eating out and being seen in public places."

"But not in front of work colleagues, or friends or family," she added quickly.

"Definitely not that. I'd get interrogated by Ralph. Not something I'm looking forward to."

"This Ralph character sounds interesting."

"You might get to meet him one day, if you're lucky."

She wondered what that would be like, and how he would introduce her. Maybe that day would never come. Maybe they would be able to keep their marriage a perfect secret until the year was up.

Are you really ok for me to stay over?" he wanted to know. "I'm being honest now, Shay. This is a huge move into uncharted territory. I'll be honest and say that this still feels surreal to me, and I don't expect this feeling to go away anytime soon. Does this feel weird to you?"

She had to laugh at that. "Do you think I take strangers into my house and marry them on a whim every day?"

"That's not what I meant, and besides, we're not strangers. We've known one another for over three years. That doesn't make you a stranger to me." The way he said it, speaking with such conviction, momentarily startled her, and she felt a little better for his words.

Feeling slightly more at ease now she asked, "What type of pizza do you like?"

"What type of pizza? Hmm. That's a question that requires as much thought as a Vegas wedding."

They laughed, then discussed their pizza toppings, eventually settling on a large pizza with ham and pineapple on one half, and a hot spicy vegetarian with olives on the other.

Talking about pizza topics had lightened the mood somewhat.

"Shall we open a bottle of wine?" she asked, once she'd placed the pizza order.

The moment she asked it, she questioned the wisdom of this. Wine would loosen her tongue, and make her more relaxed. Feeling more relaxed around Blake probably wasn't a good thing, at least until her hormones had calmed down. She was sure they would once she got over the novelty of having him suddenly be a part of her life.

"I'm heading to the gym first thing in the morning, so no wine for me, thanks."

Good, at least that solved that problem. "The gym?"

"I'll probably be out before you get up." She couldn't help but run her gaze up and down the length of his body. "You work out every week?"

"Most weekends, yes. I don't have much time to myself during the weekdays."

She forced herself to look him in the eye and not be tempted to stare at his muscles, especially since he'd now folded his arms and seemed to be deliberately showing them off. "I run sometimes, and I always go for a swim. I have to stay fit. This is the only exercise I do."

"It sounds like a lot!" She was amazed and shocked to think that a person would willingly spend time their free time in the pursuit of such painful activities.

"I do long hours at the factory, in a sedentary position. And mentally, it's hard running a business with so much riding on me. I need a way to get rid of my stress and exercise makes me feel good. You should come with me."

She balked at the idea. There was no way she would allow herself to go for a run or step into a gym with this man, because she would definitely embarrass herself.

And there was no way she would ever allow him to see her in

a swimsuit or a bikini. Her cheeks heated up. There was no way she'd be able to cope seeing him in his swim trunks.

Luckily, the sound of the doorbell put a stop to her thoughts

Sharing a pizza went well.

Having more iced tea with it worked like a charm. It felt like having a friend over. They even managed to watch TV together. It helped that it was a comedy.

If she had been home alone, or if Jenna had been here, they would have had wine, and relaxed and continued watching TV for a good few hours more.

But things were already different because it was Blake. And because it was him, and he was going to the gym, she excused herself and went to bed earlier than she ordinarily would have.

In bed she watched a film on her iPad, with her headphones plugged in. At least watching the film took her mind off the fact that the gorgeous Blake Kennedy was lying on her couch.

CHAPTER 21

It took him a while to fall asleep. The couch took some getting used to. It wasn't uncomfortable, in fact, it was enough to accommodate his long frame, and it wasn't too hard. He might feel differently after a few weeks, but comfort factor-wise, it was fine.

It was the thought of Shay being in the room nearby that kept him awake. Apart from that, the two of them were getting on well, and the earlier part of the evening had been a breeze.

He managed to catch a few hours of sleep, and then went to the gym before Shay got up. And then he stayed away for most of the day, showering at the gym and changing back into his casual clothes before heading to the factory, as he did a lot of the time on weekends, to catch up on things he never got the chance to deal with during the weekdays.

By the time he got back, it was late in the evening. He'd called Shay on his way home—on his way to her apartment, to ask if he should pick up a take out from Fellini's for her. She was happy with the takeout, and so that's what he did.

They ate, and watched a little TV and then she went to her

room and he stayed up some more and went to sleep. The second night he slept better.

There was also the question of laundry and ironing and shaving and grooming. Things he had never had to think about when he lived alone. He couldn't exactly open up an ironing board in her living room and iron away. But he could get his shirts dry-cleaned and ironed, and so he decided to make a note to do that when he had two weeks' worth of clothes that needed washing.

The rest of the following week continued much like the same. Weekdays were easier to get through, simply because his whole day was taken up at the factory. It was weekends that were harder.

They even had a system in place for weekday mornings. He'd wake up earlier than her and shower, and then she would go in and shower after him, while he made coffee for them both.

He never ate breakfast, but she had cereal. And then they would get into their cars and each drive to work, separately since they both worked in different directions.

The first week passed easily.

The following weekend, Shay woke up earlier than usual, and he was still getting changed into his gym gear, when she walked into the living room and screamed.

He was in his boxer briefs and had just put his head through a gym vest. He quickly slid down his vest. "Sorry."

Her face turned red. "I forgot you were here."

"Easy to do."

Her mouth fell open and she looked him up and down, before remembering to close her mouth again.

"I should get changed in the bathroom. I wasn't expecting you to be up so soon," he said. He was standing barefoot and looked around for his socks.

"It might be an idea," she said, and then he noticed that she was in her crop top with PJ shorts. She folded her arms, and backed away towards her bedroom door. But dang it if he hadn't already gotten a peak of her cute shorts. "Have you… do you… have you finished in the bathroom?" she asked, struggling to get a sentence together.

"I've finished." But he was curious. "Why are you up so early?"

"I'm visiting my parents. I meant to tell you last night."

He nodded. "Is everything okay with them?" He wondered why she went to see them so often.

She nodded. "I probably won't be back until really late. Sometimes I stay over."

"Okay."

They looked at one another. He tried not to let his gaze wander over her legs, or linger over her too much. Hard to keep his eyes pinned to hers.

"I'd better get to the gym."

"I'd better go and shower."

She couldn't rush into the shower fast enough.

How could she forget he was here?

It was just that he was normally awake and the living room was clear by the time she woke up.

She'd been starting to believe that this little arrangement of theirs wasn't as difficult as she been afraid of. It was like it used to be when Jenna had stayed over, only Blake was neater, and more discreet. She almost got the sense that he was doing his utmost to stay out of her way and to avoid taking up too much of her time and space.

Last weekend he'd disappeared for most of the weekend. Ordinarily she would have been away at her parent's place, but she'd stayed over on the Friday and so was at her place on the weekend. She had expected to see more of Blake but she'd barely seen him.

It seemed to her that he spent most of this time at the gym, and then the factory, but her feminine intuition made her wonder if he was using those places as an excuse to get away.

She didn't want him to feel that way.

But she appreciated that he might need a proper night's sleep, and the use of his own bathroom. She'd never seen his place and had no idea where he lived or what his place was like.

Trust Aunt Dena to put such a difficult stipulation on her— proof of a marriage, and of living with her husband.

As they tried to get used to this false living-togetherness, she realized that she hadn't even thought about the inheritance, except for the peace of mind it would bring to her regarding her father's treatment. Neither she nor Blake had talked about the money, or her Great Aunt Dena.

When the time came for them to claim the inheritance, it would also be time for things to revert back to normal, for Blake to move out and for them to get divorced. And that time seemed a long way away right now.

CHAPTER 22

Another week passed and he was getting used to this way of life. He got changed in the bathroom, then cleaned up the shower and wiped down the surfaces which he'd splashed water. Then tidied up his toiletries on the shelf. Stuff he wouldn't be so paranoid about in his own home.

Now he needed to get his clothes washed and laundered, dry-cleaned if possible. As he walked out of the bathroom and into the living room he found Shay on the floor on all fours, with her back to him. She was holding some sort of plastic sword in her hand.

"What are you doing?"

She jumped and glanced over her shoulder, and he saw something tiny and black dart across the floor.

"The darned spider," she cried. "There's a family of them in here somewhere, I seem to catch one every week."

She turned back around, and he was left with the picture of her cute behind. "Where'd it go now?" she wailed.

He was on it. He walked around her, then bent down and cupped the thing in between his hands. "This little fella?" She shrank back in fear. This surprised him. Shay Donovan was frightened of these little things? He'd never understood this irrational fear himself, given that humans were so many times bigger.

"Don't kill it!"

"Who says I'm going to kill it??" He walked over to the window, opened it and threw it out.

She stood up slowly. "You picked it up in your hands?"

He stared at the long implement in her hand. "Is that what you use to catch it?"

She nodded.

"I've seen a few spiders crawling around in here," he told her.

"A few?" she cried, as if it was a few too many.

"I'll make sure to get rid of them for you."

"You will?" If it would make things easier for her, yes he would. Come to think of it, he'd do anything to make things easier for her. Make her happier, make her smile. He was already doing that, wasn't he? With the will and the marriage? Only problem was, even just a few weeks in, he was getting to like this.

"Thanks," she said, folding her arms.

"Don't mention it. How come you're up so early?"

"I'm visiting my parents."

"You are? I mean, that's great. You seem close to them."

"They're not so far away."

"I mean close, as in wanting to spend time with them every weekend."

She didn't say anything.

"I'd better head on to the gym then. See you later or tomorrow?" he asked, remembering that she'd told him last time that she sometimes stayed over.

"I'm not sure yet."

He detected a note of questioning in that statement, as if she was testing him. "I don't need to have the place to myself."

"Are you sure?" she asked.

"I'm sure. What makes you think I need the place to myself?"

"You're hardly here at the weekend."

"That's because, as I said to you before, I spend a lot of time working out and…" And last week he'd gone for brunch and stayed out longer than he would have if he'd had his own place. Come to think of it, he needed to go and check up on his house, as he hadn't had a chance to this week.

"And?"

"I assumed you'd want some time to yourself. Me being here, in your face all the time."

"You're not in my face all the time," she contested.

"Not during the week, for obvious reasons, but weekends, I assumed you'd want some time to yourself."

"I was worried that you might feel as if you're imposing, and that's why you want to stay away. I was right."

He couldn't work out if she was sorry about this, or if she was stating a fact. But the fact that they were having this conversation meant they were both aware of one another's feelings. She was like a girlfriend, but without the romance, like a friend from whom he had to hide his feelings.

This state of affairs could confuse the heck out of a saner person.

"I don't want you to feel out of place here, Blake. You shouldn't have to stay away all day at the weekend because you're afraid of getting in my way. We had a deal, remember? And a year is a long time to spend like this."

It was a long time. She was talking about the mood and the atmosphere and their living space, but to him, the thing that had started to bother him was being around her. It was testing him, being in such a small space, talking to her, seeing her like this, in her night clothes, in her casual clothes, seeing her vulnerable, without makeup, with her hair messy—seeing all these facets of Shay for the first time.

It was hard not to be drawn to her.

He was getting to see not just the polished professional he'd always seen at the town hall meetings, but the real woman behind that persona.

"I don't feel out of place," he said, wanting to reassure her. "I really don't."

"Sure?"

"I'm sure." He didn't feel so much out of place as he did out of sorts, sometimes. Like now. They were stretching out this conversation, seemed as if they could watch TV and joke and laugh and talk about their day at work over dinner, but this type of conversation they tended to avoid. They hadn't spoken about the will, or the inheritance money, even though they sometimes joked about someone from the lawyer's office turning up to spy on them. This, right now was the closest they had come to talking about their living arrangements and being frank; arrangements that had been hastily made and hastily executed, but they were both being considerate of one another's feelings. There was no problem except an increasing awareness on his part about how he felt about her. And how careful he had to be to remain detached.

"You haven't done any washing?" she asked.

"Have you been paying close attention to my laundry habits?"

"I noticed, that's all."

He placed his hands on his hips, then, thinking that it was too defensive a stance, relaxed his arms by his sides. "I was going to get them dry-cleaned, at a store."

"Are they particularly expensive?"

"No."

"Then why don't you put them in the washing machine?"

"I didn't want to go through the hassle of ironing them and taking over the living room while you're watching TV."

"It's not a problem. You can use my washing machine and drier, and you're welcome to use the ironing board and iron. It's in the laundry closet. I'm not going to be a dutiful wife and offer to iron them for you."

Dutiful wife. He wouldn't ever expect things from his partner, but he quite liked the word *wife*, especially when Shay said it just now. "I don't expect you do my ironing for me. Even if we were really married, I'd do my own ironing. I'd probably do yours, too."

"Then it would be worth marrying you on that basis alone."

"You *have* married me," he countered with a smile.

"I mean, for real."

"Oh, for real." He smiled at the thought, and then sobered up because that scenario was so far from their current one.

"It's the monthly meeting tomorrow," he stated, remembering that it was that time of the month again, and changing the topic.

"Is it?" A look of surprise crossed her face, then something else he couldn't read easily. He wasn't sure how they would navigate the event this time around. Did they still speak to one another with the same snarkiness that was usually the flavor of their past conversations? Or did they behave the way they were towards one another now; friendly, curious and as good friends?

"One of us could miss it?" he suggested, thinking it would be easier that way.

"Jenna says Reed's giving us all an update about the opening of his new movie theater and she says he has an important announcement to make.

"An important announcement?" Reed had told him the building work was finished, and he was interested to hear the businessman's plans for it.

"We should both go, as usual," Shay suggested. "We can't miss every meeting every month for the next year."

True." One big lie was resulting in so many tiny little ones already. One day, he was certain, they would all catch up.

CHAPTER 23

She had spent the entire day at her parents' house. The shadow scare was over with and they could breathe easy. It had been nothing serious.

Her father seemed to have a little more energy, and her mother seemed more relaxed than Shay had observed in weeks.

Understandably so.

Shay cooked dinner, and helped out as much as she could so that her mother got some time to unwind.

They were both disappointed when she told them she couldn't stay the night, but she had arranged to meet Jenna tomorrow.

And also, knowing that Blake was in her apartment made her want to go back. Not because she didn't trust him. She did.

"I won't leave right after dinner," she'd said, wanting to pacify them, and so she'd stayed later than usual and ended up arriving back at midnight.

This visit had been great. She hadn't come back fearful about her father's prospects, and the doctors had said that he was responding well to the treatment. She felt happier than usual as she walked into her apartment and turned on the light.

When something moved, then sat up, she screamed. Then put

her hand to her mouth as she saw Blake, lying shirtless on her couch, with the duvet falling to his waist.

"Sorry," she cried, and tried not to look at his bare chest. "I forgot." It wasn't that she had completely erased from her mind that he lived here, but that there were still moments when she didn't expect him to be here, like now. He still took her by surprise.

Only, this time, she wasn't sure what scared her more; the unexpected shock of seeing Blake stretched out on her couch, or the fact that he was shirtless. He got up, revealing only boxer briefs and she dropped her keys in shock.

"Could you ...could you put something on?" she asked, averting her gaze and bending down to pick up her keys.

"Sorry. I waited up for you, and only went to sleep a short while ago. I didn't think you were coming back tonight."

She still looked away, not trusting herself to stare in his direction. Blake fully clothed had been the last thought in her mind as she often lay down to sleep. But Blake in his boxer briefs only would be more than her system could handle.

"I stayed late but I had planned to return."

He moved his duvet out of the way. "I'm decent now," he said, injecting a small laugh into his words. She made herself look at him. Blake looking slightly disheveled, with his hair all messed up, barefoot and in sweatpants and a T-shirt now was more than her body could handle.

Her heartrate started to climb.

It didn't matter whether this man was partially or fully clothed; he was increasingly looking more delicious with each passing day.

"How were your parents?" he asked.

"They were fine." She was still standing by the door and the empty space between them was filled with something sizzling; something electric. She hadn't experienced anything like this before—some invisible feeling that she couldn't see, touch or feel, but which she could sense because it made her insides go dizzy. She wasn't sure what to do, whether to take a step forward and close the distance between them, or to just sit down. Or maybe even walk right past him and go to sleep. Only, he looked as if he'd rolled up his duvet and was waiting for something.

He looked as if he had no intention of sleeping. And this suited her fine because she was wide awake and had no intention of sleeping either.

"Why don't you sit down?" he asked, breaking the silence.

"It's late. Don't you want to sleep?"

"I'm wide awake now. I wouldn't be able to fall asleep easily if I tried.

"Sorry." She felt bad for waking him.

"Don't be."

She took off her jacket, and walked awkwardly to the couch. "How was your day?"

"I managed to get all my washing and ironing done."

"Now that's a result."

"I took your advice."

"Good."

They sat in silence for a few more seconds, and she tried to think of something to say. Usually their conversations were effortless, but tonight, the conversation was stilted.

It seemed that seeing him shirtless had short circuited her brain.

"Did you say you waited up for me?" The thought of that gave her a feeling of belonging. It was new, and unexpected, and his words had latched deep in her core because it was a novelty, to have someone be there for her like this.

"I wasn't sure of what your plans were, so I watched a film. I couldn't sleep anyway."

"Which one?"

"The Da Vinci Code."

"I love that film! Have you seen the one after? Angels and Demons?"

"No. Do you want to see it?" he asked.

It wasn't as if she was going to get any sleep any time soon. "We could, I suppose." She was wide awake as well, and it was only a little after midnight.

"Okay, I'll get it ready," he told her.

"I'll get changed."

"Changed?"

"Into my PJs."

A short while later, they were sitting on the couch with an empty space between them, watching a movie way after midnight.

CHAPTER 24

"I'll meet you there," she'd told Blake when they'd left for work in the morning. Now she was back at the town hall, at the monthly meeting, catching up with Jenna who was making sure there was enough on the refreshment table.

It seemed like a déjà vu moment from last month.

Except that this was real, not imagined, and the smartly dressed man across the room from her, deep in conversation with Reed and his friends, was her husband.

Had he always been so smartly dressed, or did he just happen to look more and more sexy, and good looking to her every day?

"Don't you want to know?" Jenna asked, loud enough to pull her attention off Blake.

"Know what?"

"You haven't been listening," Jenna complained. "And why are you checking out Rourke again?"

"I am not!" Shay insisted. She might have done so in the past, but she was ogling the tall dark and handsome grey-eyed man next to him.

Her man.

If only.

"I'm not stupid, Shay," her friend insisted. She finished rearranging the donuts on the plate. "But you're too late for Rourke."

"I'm not interested in Rourke, and I'm *not* eyeballing him. What were you saying?" she asked, eager to lead the conversation in another direction. "Don't I want to know what?"

"The movie theater. Reed's making an announcement about it."

"I know. It's finished and ready to open."

"That's not the announcement," Jenna retorted.

"He's having an opening night, I heard." Blake had hinted at such a thing, and since he and Reed knew one another, she was inclined to believe what Blake told her.

"That's not all." Jenna's eyes glinted with wickedness. She looked like a child bursting to let out a secret.

"Then what?"

"You'll have to wait and see."

"You can be so annoying sometimes!" Shay caught Blake giving her an ill-concealed smiled. Her insides lit up like fireflies on a dark sultry night.

"We need more donuts," said Jenna, thankfully, and turned to leave.

"I'll catch up with you at the end," said Shay. Blake was making his way towards her and she suddenly felt a rush of adrenaline shoot through her veins.

"I was hoping you'd have your back turned to me so that I could surprise you like last time," he said, coming to a stop in front of her.

"I'm not touching another banana."

"It's still possible to choke on a donut," he reasoned.

"I don't intend to choke at all tonight, so there will be no need for you to save my life all over again."

He lifted his eyebrow. "It doesn't matter because I have the reward I was looking for," he said, his voice almost a whisper. She wasn't sure exactly what he meant by this. "Reward? You won't get that for a year."

"You," he said, the one word rendering her completely speechless.

Her lips parted. Did he mean what she thought he meant? Was he feeling what she felt? "Me?"

She dared not say another word and tried to enjoy this second's worth of happiness.

"Reed's having a grand opening night for the movie theater. Last time I didn't have a plus one to bring along, but I can now."

"I'm not your plus one." She looked around her, knowing that it was wrong of them to even have this type of conversation here where there were so many ears, and so much potential for their secret to be revealed, and yet, she couldn't help herself.

"Live a little, Shay."

What was he talking about? "We're supposed to keep this under wraps," she reminded him. He already knew that, so why was he suggesting that she accompany him to the movie night and draw even more attention to them?

"It was only a suggestion. It's not a big deal," he said, defensively. "Sometimes you tend to overthink things."

"Me? Over think things?" That was rich. "Did it ever occur to you that we have to be careful about certain situations? How can I be your plus one?" It was difficult trying to keep her voice low when she was outraged about making such an important point. How had he forgotten this already? And at a place like this—a public place where they were both going to be seen together?

It was tricky, trying to behave like a married couple for prying eyes, and at the same time try and appear as if they were nothing more than mere acquaintances to friends. The balance was almost impossible, but then so was this situation. She was in it now. *They* were in it, and they had no choice but to make the most of it.

He looked away, as if he'd grown bored of her conversation. "Blake," she whispered. "How were you expecting to explain you and me going together? We've talked about keeping this to ourselves," she hissed, lowering her voice to a whisper. "Why would you suggest it?"

"I heard you the first time," he replied, his voice decidedly harder. "I wasn't thinking properly, Shay. Sometimes I forget what our status is and who's supposed to know what."

The irritation in his voice made her stop and ponder. He couldn't have forgotten their arrangement, and their secret. And she didn't understand why he was making out as if he had.

"There you are." Francine joined them, interrupting their conversation.

"If you could come up with suitable candidates by October, that will give me plenty of time to review them," Blake said to Shay, smoothly covering up the nature of their conversation.

"I have a few possible candidates," she replied. She had relayed Blake's request to Francine, but hadn't, as yet, done anything about seeking out staff to temporarily fill the maternity leave requirements at his work place.

"If you'll excuse me," said Blake, moving away.

"What a surprise to see you both," Francine commented, drily.

"We were talking about the staffing issues at his factory."

"Still? You seem to talk about that a lot," Francine observed. "Quite odd, given that those positions don't have to be filled for a few months yet."

"You know me and Blake," said Shay, snorting a small laugh. "What else do we have to talk about if not work?" She could feel Francine observing her, but Shay chose to look away and then pretended to be busy checking the messages on her phone.

CHAPTER 25

They sat apart, deliberately.

Shay had already hinted, when Francine left them, that they were being different around one another and she was sure that Francine could tell.

"Nonsense!" he'd cried, then leaned in to her ear. "How on earth would she think we were married just because we were having a civil conversation for a change?"

She'd shivered. He had actually seen her shiver. "What's wrong?" he asked, moving his head away.

"You… you… tickled my neck."

He'd been nowhere near her neck. But he wasn't going to dispute it.

They stood quietly as the minutes stretched out uncomfortably before them. Then, just like that, Shay announced that she was going to go and take a seat. He was about to join her, when she hissed. "I'm sitting with Francine. You can't sit with me," she hissed. "We never sit together."

"I gave you the Heimlich maneuver. It's not illogical to assume that we'd be on better terms after such a bonding experience."

"We're not supposed to draw attention to ourselves. We don't want friends to know."

While he sometimes enjoyed teasing her, and was always ready to listen to her excuses and paranoia when he suggested they do things together, there were times where it got annoying. Because she was clearly using every excuse in the book for them not to be seen together, where, in his opinion, this amount of conversation, and change in their dynamics, and even—surprise surprise—the two of them sitting together—was perfectly normal.

But Shay was behaving as if this was anything but normal.

In this they differed.

On deeper reflection, it seemed to him a sign that his feelings for Shay were deepening too quickly, while her feelings towards him hadn't changed at all. She didn't care for him, didn't think of him the way he thought of her, and he would do well to remember that their union was founded on a purely financial whim.

So lost was he in this quagmire of thoughts that when the whole room collectively gasped, and a silence fell, he had no idea what it was in reaction to.

Reed was on stage and talking. This must have been the announcement he'd been keen to hear, but he'd missed it all.

"*The* Hailey Ross?" someone asked.

Reed laughed. "Yes, *the* Hailey Ross. Starling Bay's very own Hollywood star."

Talk about a major announcement.

"Hailey Ross's latest Hollywood film will have a second premiere here in Starling Bay, at the newly remodelled Knight Movie Theater and she will be here for that event."

"When?" someone else asked.

"That's an announcement for another day." Reed grinned as the murmurs spread around the excited audience. "But, she's definitely coming, folks. She's returning for a reason. You can ask her about it all when you next see her."

Hailey Ross had been a starlet when she'd left Starling Bay for the lights of Hollywood, and after starring successfully in many children's TV shows, she'd made the huge leap into films, surprising many with her last few movie hits. She was now a huge star, and she was returning to Starling Bay. Reed Knight really did know all the right people.

This cemented his decision to attend the grand opening night. He'd have to see what Shay had to say about it.

At her request, he had sat a few rows behind her, and ended up talking to the people he was sitting with. That was the beauty of these informal meetings. Everyone was friendly, and he almost always learned something new whether it was about a new business starting up, or a change in an existing business.

Tonight's news was huge—he wasn't interested in celebrities, but he wondered if Shay might be.

As the night ended, he continued his conversation with the people he'd been sitting near, but he kept looking out for Shay, hoping to catch her eye and see what time she wanted to leave.

They'd come in separate cars, but as it was getting late, and neither of them were going to be in the mood to cook, he was going to suggest that they eat out. After her earlier paranoia about attending the grand opening night of the movie theater together, he wasn't entirely sure that his idea to have dinner together at a restaurant would go down well, but he would remind her that the person from the lawyer's office could sweep upon them at any time, and this might be a good opportunity for them to be seen out in the public eye.

He waited for her patiently, and from time to time found someone he knew gravitate towards him. Almost three quarters of an hour had passed, and Shay was happily engaged in conversation. She was chatting with Reed and his friends, along with Francine. A large crowd had surrounded Reed, which didn't surprise him. He was certain they all had questions about Hailey Ross.

At last Shay walked over to him. "What are you still doing here?"

The question surprised him. "I was waiting for you."

"Why? We came in different cars." She sounded irritated, and all he'd done was be considerate.

"Would you rather I left without telling you?" Maybe he should have left, given her mood.

"But we never go home together."

"I was being polite, Shay." He had to school himself to stay calm, because something about her question and the way in which she'd asked it, annoyed the heck out of him.

Her expression softened. "I didn't mean it like that."

"You sound as if you want me gone."

"No, that's not true," she insisted.

He glanced at the dwindling crowd around him. "I don't understand why you're being so uptight. Nobody's watching us, and nobody thinks anything of you and me talking. I can assure you that nobody thinks we're together."

She shot daggers at him. "Look, Blake. I don't know how we're supposed to behave."

"Like normal people."

She shook her head. "I can't compartmentalize what we are."

"Then don't."

"I don't know how to reconcile what we've been in the past and what we're trying to be now."

"I'm not trying to be anything, Shay."

"That's not true. You're supposed to be my husband, but you and I know this is a lie."

"I'm not trying to be your husband, Shay, I'm trying to be your friend."

"Are you two still here?" Francine had suddenly appeared by their side, and Shay looked as if she'd seen not one ghost, but ten.

"I was helping Jenna clean up," said Shay.

"I'm going home," said Francine, and nodded at them both.

"I'll see you tomorrow." Shay looked slightly embarrassed.

"She didn't hear," he said, wanting to reassure her as soon as her boss was out of earshot.

"How do you know?"

"Because I was talking in a low voice," he replied, trying to reassure her.

"She's got bionic ears."

"You think everyone's got bionic ears," he pointed out.

"You're too laid back," she accused.

"You're too uptight."

"Reed's invited me to the grand opening night," he said, not wanting them to have what threatened to become their first major disagreement.

"And Jenna's invited me," she replied, looking not very happy.

"So we're both going?" he asked.

"I'm going, and you can if you want to."

"I really don't understand why we can't go together."

"Blake!"

Because he wasn't ready to end the night on a sour note, he made the suggestion which had been bubbling up inside him.

"How about we go for something to eat? Neither of us will be in the mood to cook when we get home."

"To get something to eat?"

"We did it before, at The Olive Tree. You didn't think it was such a big deal for us to be seen in public together that night—"

"But we weren't married then."

"Exactly, and no one knows that we are now, so what difference does it make?"

He seemed to have gotten through to her because she stopped and appeared to consider his suggestion.

"We could go back there again?" she suggested.

"We can go wherever you want. I'm starving."

"Me too."

CHAPTER 26

$\mathcal{I}$t turned out that they'd had a lovely meal, and she was pleasantly surprised. The evening had ended on a more relaxed note than that with which it had begun. Her initial reaction to Blake's suggestion to have dinner together had been to turn it down, but that was only because tonight's meeting had demonstrated just how much her feelings for Blake had changed.

Where once he had been the object of her friendly sarcasm and had never registered on her radar—that position being solely occupied by Rourke for many years—now things had turned full circle.

She hadn't been interested in Rourke ever since she'd learned that he was quite serious, and quite in love with his latest girlfriend.

But it was Blake whom she was beginning to see with new eyes, a new heart, and new feelings. Feelings which both surprised her and scared her to the point that she was confused about them.

Had she come to have these romantic feelings about Blake because he was a kind and considerate friend who was willing to help her out; and because he was also increasingly good looking, too? Or was it because she was getting used to his easy company, and because she was lonely, and because her apartment was no longer empty and because he was funny, and warm, and giving?

As she wrestled with these thoughts and feelings, which had come to the surface this evening, she was on high alert.

She never had to think about Blake and their situation at work much, and in the safety and privacy of her apartment these things didn't matter. It was only the little white lies which she had to occasionally tell her parents, and Francine, and Jenna. Her friend had called a number of times and asked if she could come over so that they could catch up but so far, Shay had managed to stall her.

Tonight she had been even more on edge than usual. Things weren't made any easier because as uptight as she had been, Blake had been the opposite.

She'd very nearly not accepted his invite to dinner, until he had reminded her that it would be a chance for them to be seen together, not in the presence of friends or family, but hopefully seen by someone from the lawyer's office.

They'd gone to a quiet little restaurant not on the main beachfront, but along one of the side streets.

There, in the privacy of a half-empty dining place, she'd felt able to relax. And now, as she sat across the table from him, feeling happier, and sated with a good meal, she felt even more relaxed.

They joked about Hyacinth who hadn't looked too happy this evening. Shay was explaining the reason why.

"She had wrongly assumed that Reed was going to name the movie theater after her."

Blake slammed down his glass of water. "She's already got The Fitzsimmons Theater."

"Be that as it may, she expected Reed to call the movie theater The Fitzsimmons Movie Theater. And he didn't. He named it after himself which is only fitting."

"And she found out and didn't like it?" Blake guessed.

"She found out that he'd named the pizzeria after her. Fitzsimmons Pizzeria."

They laughed together at that. "There's a pizzeria in the movie theater?"

Shay nodded. "Jenna says there isn't just hotdogs and popcorn to buy, but a pizza parlor, an ice cream parlor and a whole food court with various food and drink. It's meant to be real pretty."

"That man doesn't do things by half, and it was still generous of him to name the pizzeria after Hyacinth. He didn't need to," said Blake.

"My thoughts, exactly."

"I hope she doesn't take it out on Jenna, what with her working for her."

"Jenna's more than capable of looking after herself."

"Shall I get the bill?" he asked, looking eager to go. She'd been about to suggest that they have some coffee, but since he seemed ready to leave, she decided against it.

"I've got an early start tomorrow," he explained.

She went to get her purse, but he insisted on paying. "How would it look to others," he said.

"My turn next time."

"We ought to hold hands or something," he suggested, jokingly as they left the restaurant, and because she was in such a good mood, she didn't put up a fight. Their hands easily slipped together into a light touch, No fingers entwining, just his palm on hers.

But it was enough. It felt nice. Comforting. Normal. Blake was right. She did tend to overthink things.

"What if someone sees us?" she whispered.

"Isn't that the idea?" he asked. "Don't you want the likes of your lawyer friend to see us?"

He had a valid point, although the chances of that happening were close to zero.

So they continued to walk through the streets of the bay, holding hands and looking very much like a couple who were in love.

The dinner seemed to have taken the edge off the tensions that had come up during the town hall meeting.

Walking back towards where their cars were parked, she allowed herself for one indulgent moment, to get carried away, and to imagine that she was with him, that this was real, and there was nothing underhanded about their being together.

They were beginning to fit together like a glove.

And even when they arrived home, they watched TV together for a while, before she retired to her bedroom. Then she lay in bed, unable to sleep for a while, thinking of Blake in the next room, and the absurdity of their life.

If this were real, he'd be lying in bed next to her. Holding her even. Kissing her, and more. She'd started to wonder what it might feel like, to have his lips pressed on hers, to have his arms wrapped around her waist, to feel his body against hers.

These thoughts didn't help her to sleep in any way; they made every new morning a little harder to be around him. She was thankful for the weekdays when she could go to work, when they were out of one another's way for the entire day.

She was still visiting her parents at the weekend, but didn't stay over anymore. It was nice and comforting to know that Blake was at home waiting for her. Maybe not exactly *waiting* for her, but she liked the idea that he was there.

They had settled into an effortless routine, and she was beginning to get used to it. Thoughts of the end of their year together were increasingly pushed to the back of her mind.

With a shock it struck her that it would be their one-month anniversary in a few days' time.

How fast the time had flown.

There was no doubt in her mind that the rest of the year would whizz by just as fast, and she felt a tiny pinch in her belly at the thought.

She considered mentioning their anniversary to him, to see his reaction, then thought better of it. What was there to celebrate? He'd think she was being too romantic, which would be a change from him accusing her of over thinking matters.

It had crept up on her slowly, that Blake's opinion of her mattered. That she cared what he thought, of her, how he saw her, but most of all, she wondered—while keeping her own conflicted feelings under wraps—if he harbored any such feelings for her.

Sometimes he looked at her, and they both stared at one another a little longer than was usual, and sometimes, her gaze slid to his lips. She'd noticed he'd done that too. And once or twice, when they'd sat down to watch TV on the couch, they'd sat too close, their arms or legs almost brushing together, before they moved apart, as if touched by a spark of electricity.

These little things always made her wonder, and she wished for the gift of telepathy so that she could climb inside his brain and find out what he really thought of her.

As it was, on the surface of it, Blake was the perfect gentleman. He was so good, he might as well have been a monk. No more did he get changed in the living room, and she hardly ever saw him lying in the couch under the duvet. He was always up and out of the way before she was up.

Secretly, she'd been hoping for another glimpse of his chest.

It seemed she had nothing better to do than to torture herself.

With work, and staying in touch with her parents, as well as keeping a close eye on her dad's progress, she had more than enough things to keep her mind off Blake and her increasingly complicated living situation.

Jenna had called a few times this week, prompting Shay to

wonder if something was up with her and Reed. She'd told her that they could meet on Sunday because she planned to see her parents the day before.

Were there problems in love land for Jenna and Reed? Shay could think of no other reason for her friend's insistence to meet up.

But when her doorbell rang one evening in the middle of the week, Shay opened the door to find Jenna grinning at her.

"Surprise!" she cried out, opening her arms wide as if she'd climbed out of a huge birthday cake.

"Jenna?" she cried, in shock. Her mind raced to the state of the living room, to the tell-tale signs of Blake living here. It was too late to shut the door now that Jenna was standing there looking at her with glee. "What are you doing here?"

"Thanks for the wonderful welcome," said Jenna, her expression slightly deflated.

Shay froze, wondering how to get out of this. Blake wasn't at home yet, but how awkward it would be if he arrived now. How would she explain herself out of that situation?

"Aren't you going to ask me in?"

Shay started getting palpitations, but there was nothing she could do. "I was on my way out," she replied, thinking of the first thing that came to mind.

"Yeah? Where to?"

"I … I needed to pick up a few things for dinner."

"Yeah?" Jenna folded her arms. "What are you making?"

She was stumped. "Pasta."

"What are you hiding?" Jenna asked.

Shay laughed, perhaps a little too louder than normal. "What? What do you mean?"

"There's nothing you want to tell me?" her friend insisted, not moving an inch.

"No."

"So there's no reason you're not letting me in?"

Shay lifted her chin, pondering what to do. "Come in," she said, finally.

Jenna stepped boldly through the door.

"Is there something going on with you?" Shay asked, knowing of no other reason why her friend would turn up on her doorstep like this, unannounced and out of the blue.

"Is there something going on with *you?*" Jenna asked.

"What?" Shay laughed again. "No!" Then, "Are you and Reed having problems?" She tried to deflect the conversation away from Jenna's line of inquiry.

"No. Reed and I are fine. We're great, in fact. I've been trying to get together with you and I noticed that you've been avoiding me."

"That's not true", Shay insisted, knowing this to be completely true. "We saw one another only a few days ago."

"About that," said Jenna. "Care to tell me what you and Blake Kennedy were doing holding hands?"

Shay's palms turned clammy, and she tried to deny it. "Holding hands? Me and Blake?" She tried to inject a touch of indignation into her voice, but it was a half–hearted attempt which fell flat.

"Yes, you and Blake Kennedy—the man you loved to hate, the man you said always made it a point to annoy the heck out of you at every town hall meeting."

"When did you see us?"

"After you left the restaurant. We saw you two leave. We'd gone to Fellini's after finishing up at the meeting, and we'd gone for a walk by the beach."

She'd been caught red-handed and there was no way out of this. What could she tell her, and how much could she get away with?

"So?" asked Jenna. She didn't sound annoyed, or look

annoyed, judging by the huge grin on her face. "You don't deny it, then?"

"Is this why you've been hounding me on the phone?"

"Yes! I gave you every opportunity to confess! How could you keep this from me, Shay? I thought we were friends!"

"We *are* friends, it's not that."

Jenna clapped her hands together. "I don't believe it. You've been holding out on me for a long time."

"What? No! No, that is not true."

"You're keeping so quiet about it. You hid it from me. And if we hadn't seen you together, we would never have known."

"Does Reed know?"

"He's not blind. He saw you. He was curious why Blake hadn't said anything to him, but men don't dissect these things the way we women do. He's given it no further thought, unlike me," said Jenna, grinning mischievously.

Her friend's effervescent reaction to this situation was beginning to grate on her nerves. It was bad enough their secret getting out, but if she now owned up to the truth could she convince Jenna to keep it a secret? With Reed knowing as well, this would soon be common knowledge among their small circle of friends.

"Are those…" Jenna looked in the direction of the chest of drawers. "His sneakers?"

Tucked away in corner, though obviously not discretely enough, were Blake's large sized sneakers.

Shay panicked, wondering how to play this. Could she make out that this was something recent, something new, something not so serious? All of these things were true, and yet, they didn't make up the entire truth.

"He goes to the gym on weekends."

Jenna looked up in shock, her eyes almost ready to bug out of their sockets. Her eagle-eyes scoured the room, taking in his newspaper, and magazines, only a few, neatly lined up and placed on top of the chest of drawers.

"He stays *here?*"

"Huh?"

"How long have you two been seeing one another?" Jenna cried, looking shocked.

"Don't say it like that," Shay replied, feeling uneasy now. She didn't know what to divulge and what to hold back on.

"I'm happy for you, but I don't understand why you've kept it such a huge secret. Is he married?"

"What? No!"

"Then why the suspense? He's a gorgeous guy, Shay, I'm surprised you've only noticed him now."

Shay rubbed her hands together trying to think of something to say, but she heard the key turn in the door, and her heart thumped even louder. "You've spent so long with your eyes on Rourke Halloran that you missed seeing anyone else!" Jenna cried.

Shay squeezed her eyes shut because, in the next moment, Blake had stepped through the door and was standing there, staring at them both in shock.

"Hi," he said, somehow fixing his composure within seconds.

"You're living together?" Jenna mouthed at her, as Blake turned his back to them to close the door.

Shay's voice failed.

"What's that about Rourke Halloran?" Blake asked, facing them again. He looked mildly amused. Jenna's mouth fell open. Shay stared back at him and wished she could disappear. She looked at her friend and could see the mountain of questions on her friend's face. There was no way on earth she could explain herself out of this situation.

"Hi!" Jenna's chirpy and delayed greeting—louder than usual —seemed too much given the circumstances.

Blake nodded. "I didn't know we had company." Blake looked at her, as if he wasn't sure what to do next. Shay remained rooted to the spot, and mercifully, it was Jenna who spoke next, with the three magic words. "I should go. We'll have to catch up soon," she said, moving in for a hug. "You have lots to explain."

"Nice meeting you," she nodded at Blake as she walked past him.

He smiled in return.

Jenna saw herself out, and when the door closed, she and Blake stared at one another.

"She saw us holding hands that night after we left the restaurant."

"And she came here, armed with that information?"

"She's been calling me all week. I knew she was after something." Shay pulled out the hair grip from her ponytail, letting her hair cascade all over her shoulders. She pushed up her glasses, contemplating what she was going to say when she next met her friend. Jenna would have questions galore.

Are you living together?

How was she supposed to answer that?

She groaned, then collapsed onto the couch in despair, not wanting to risk telling Jenna anything. A moment later, Blake was by her side. "Hey," he said, his voice soft and gentle. "It's going to be fine. This was going to happen sooner or later. Someone was going to find out. We should be thankful it's your friend and not your parents, or mine.

"*Fine?* You think this is *fine?*"

"It could be worse."

"Next you'll tell me to stop over-thinking things again."

He grinned.

"She thinks we're living together."

"There's no other conclusion she could draw from it, given the circumstances."

"Do you want to tell her?" Blake asked.

"Tell her what?" She wouldn't know where to start. There was so much that was a secret, Aunt Dena's will, the stipulations of the inheritance, the marriage, the year-long living arrangement. None of these would be easy for the other person to absorb and understand.

"Do you need to tell her anything?" Blake asked.

She snapped her head towards him. "You really don't understand women, do you?"

"Can't say I've had that much experience with them."

She was intrigued about this and wanted to know more, but now was not the time to ask these types of questions. "Jenna will arrange to meet me at work tomorrow, she'll hound me until I give in and then she'll demand to know everything."

"Everything?"

"Everything." She was sure of it. "What do I tell her?"

"Tell her as much as you feel comfortable telling."

"Do I tell her we live together?"

"I'm not sure. That will open another can of worms, and you'll have to make up more lies to hide the truth."

They looked at one another for a moment. "You'll think of something, Shay, just don't over think it," he said, getting up.

"Don't overthink it?" she cried out. "My best friend has only just found out that you and I are dating, and she's seen you walk into my apartment as if you live here, what's she to think?"

"If you consider that what she's seen is so far from the truth, I'm sure you'll find a way to convince her of anything."

She was still worried. It was easy enough for him to brush it off. He'd be singing a different tune if that was his parents, or sister, or that nosey foreman of his.

"Shay," he said, crouching on the floor, and looking at her. Her breath stopped and stuck in her throat. His gray eyes bore into hers, and he touched her knees. She flinched internally, amazed that he could stay so calm, not only because of what had happened with Jenna, but because he had no idea how that simple motion, his hands on her knees was at once friendly, and comforting, yet setting off fireworks inside her.

If he'd hoped to reassure her, his touch was doing the exact opposite.

"Just see her tomorrow, and get it over and done with."

She knew she'd have to. "I might meet with her after work."

"After work?" He frowned. "She could be pestering you for hours. It might be better to meet her at lunchtime, then you at least have the excuse to get back to work should you need to get away from her questioning."

Smart man. "You understand women better than you think you do."

CHAPTER 27

*J*enna had hunted her down.

They met at Roxy's for lunch, and this way Shay knew she had an hour at most.

"So," said Jenna, clasping her hands together.

"I thought we were having lunch?" Shay asked, although she knew the food wasn't the reason they were meeting.

"I'm having a hot chocolate. You can get what you want, but spill the beans. I want to know everything. How you met, when you met. All the details."

Shay had been rehearsing this in her mind all morning. She wasn't going to mention anything about Aunt Dena's will, or the inheritance, or the fake marriage, or the year of living together. She had to be careful in what she said, and more importantly, she had to make sure that it was believable to her friend.

So she told her that she'd noticed Blake, because it was hard not to notice a man with dark hair and gray eyes. As she spoke, she kicked herself, and wondered why she hadn't noticed him long before she had been forced into taking him into consideration.

"But did he notice you?"

"He saved me from choking on the banana."

"You guys got together from that moment?"

Shay nodded.

"And now you're living together?" Jenna cried, incredulous.

"Shhhh" hissed Shay, putting her finger to her mouth. They ordered two hot chocolates when the server came over, and Shay placed an order for a sandwich to go. "We are not living together," she insisted.

"But his clothes, and the chest of drawers—"

"He's having some building work done at his place, and he needed to stay somewhere for a little while."

"A little while?" asked Jenna pointedly, as if she was fishing for time accurate to the nearest minute.

"He'll be gone soon."

"How long has he been at your place?"

"A week." The little white lies were adding up fast.

"One week and he gets a closet to himself?" Jenna wasn't buying it. "I lived with you for months and I didn't get a closet to myself."

"That's because he doesn't want to walk in on me getting dressed. It was different with you. He sleeps on the couch, and I sleep in my room. It's all above board."

"Is he a good kisser?" Jenna asked.

Shay blushed, which only made her friend squeal louder. "On my goodness, look at your face! He *is* a great kisser. I knew it! I knew it! Those lips, those eyes… it's no wonder you want to keep him to yourself."

Shay felt herself blush. Lately, she had started to wonder what it might feel like to make out with Blake for hours. Being called out on it by her friend made her feel like a criminal. She was caught up in such an intricate web of lies that she was certain she'd mess up soon.

She turned quiet when the server returned with their hot chocolates, and a paper bag with her sandwich.

"Well?" asked Jenna impatiently. "Is he a good kisser?"

She ground down on her teeth. "Yes."

"Awwww," she squealed, like a five year old. "We should go out for dinner, you and Blake and me and Reed."

"No" she replied so fast and with such conviction that Jenna stopped and blinked. "Not yet," she replied, forcing a smile. It would be too much. *This* was too much, and Jenna was her friend. Having the four of them getting together would be torture of the highest order. Blake would find it impossible. "It's still early days, we're not... we're not completely willing to tell anyone yet."

Jenna snorted. "You're not willing to tell anyone...why? What's he hiding?"

"Nothing! He's...sensitive..."

"Sensitive?" Jenna guffawed loudly. "That's the last thing I'd expect him to be."

"He's not weak," Shay retorted quickly, not wanting to hear a bad word against Blake. "He likes keeping his personal life private. And it's complicated with him staying at my place. People will get the wrong idea."

"If it was only for a week, I don't understand why he didn't stay at a hotel. It's not like Starling Bay doesn't have any."

Shay swallowed and put up her defenses. It wouldn't surprise her if Jenna wasn't one hundred percent satisfied with what Shay had told her.

"We're going to the movie night opening," she said, hoping to add more conviction to her story.

"As a couple, or in hiding?"

She wasn't sure. That was a topic she'd bring up with Blake tonight, but she was wary because of the way she had reacted when he had suggested it before. Now, she found herself liking the idea of it. Part of it was due to the fact that all of this lying was exhausting, and the other part was that each time Blake came home, she felt a little giddy, a little more self-conscious, a little more jittery when he was around.

She was falling for him and trying to deny it.

"I can't believe you didn't tell me," said Jenna shaking her head.

"It's not as if you told me about you and Reed at the beginning."

"That was complicated. He was engaged, and there were feelings, at first. *My* feelings, I had no idea what he thought."

This seemed to be her problem as well. Shay was intrigued to find out more about them. "How did you know?"

"Know what?"

"That he felt something for you?" she asked, sitting back and cupping her hand around the hot chocolate.

"I wasn't sure. It was a hunch. My skin would prickle each time he walked past me, and then I'd catch him staring at me, and then he'd look away. It's hard to describe, but our situation was a lot different to yours. We didn't move as fast as you and Blake have." There was a mischievous glint in her eyes when she smiled.

"It's not what you think," Shay replied. "It really isn't. It's all very innocent, and pure."

"Pure?" Jenna's eyes opened wide. "How does it work then, taking showers and getting changed? You ever seen him with a towel wrapped around his waist?"

She hadn't, but now that Jenna had planted that image in her mind, it was going to be hard to shake. "It is nothing like what you're imagining in that filthy little mind of yours. It's all very innocent and sweet."

"Why do I have the feeling that there's something you're not telling me?" asked Jenna.

Shay turned on her brightest most beguiling smile and lifted her cup to her lips. "I've told you as much as you need to know. Please don't go broadcasting this to everyone," she pleaded, suddenly turning serious. She recalled that Jenna now had Reed's circle of friends that she mixed with. It wasn't that she cared about what Rourke thought. He'd been the furthest thing from her mind, but she didn't want her and Blake's business being talked about in town.

"I won't tell a soul," said Jenna. "And trust me, Reed's not interested. He thinks it's sweet, you and Blake getting together. *I* think it's sweet. And, besides, he likes Blake. They're friends, sort of."

If Jenna had more questions, she didn't ask anything more. Instead, they talked about the movie night opening which was a week away. It was going to be Starling Bay's main event, though there was going to be another event a few weeks later when Hailey Ross returned to Starling Bay.

They talked about the opening night and what to wear. It was a good thing that she'd met with Jenna today, otherwise she might have turned up in her work clothes. Instead, she'd learned that it was a black tie affair and that cocktail dresses and smart suits for the men were the order of the day. There would be champagne and canapes, as well as the reporters from the local paper covering the event.

It sounded like it was going to be a big night.

Shay found herself looking forward to it, and the idea of Blake accompanying her made her stomach flutter for no reason.

CHAPTER 28

He'd cancelled the booking at Fellini's after seeing how Shay had been worried when her friend had found out. Instead, tonight, on their one-month anniversary, he'd cooked her a meal.

"What's this?" she asked.

He spun around, and turned down the stove. "You're early. I wasn't expecting you home yet."

The kitchen was full of pots and pans by the time she got in from work. He hadn't managed to clear up yet.

"But what's this?"

"I'm cooking."

"I can see."

"Don't worry," he said, rushing towards her, as if him standing in her way might block out the sight of the mess behind him. "You look stressed, don't be. I'll take care of this."

"But what's all this?" she asked, her eyes darting around the kitchen. There was only one way to wipe that stressed expression from her face. He poured her a glass of red wine. "Here," he said, handing it to her. "Unwind. Dinner will be ready in about thirty minutes. It's our anniversary, or had you forgotten?"

She gasped. "You remembered?"

"I wouldn't forget."

"And you made all this?" she asked, her tone indicating a level of surprise which made him smile.

"I had booked at table at Fellini's."

"For our anniversary?"

"It's only a month, not a big deal, I know, but still, it's a milestone."

She looked suddenly happier, and her earlier displeasure about the mess had dissolved. She took a sip of the wine. "This is good."

"It's Australian."

"It's really good."

"I'm glad you like it."

"This is… this is so sweet of you," she said, her voice full of gratitude. She set the wine glass down and raised her hands, throwing them into the air as if she was overcome with too much emotion, too much gratitude and didn't know what to do next. For a moment it looked to him as if she was going to rush towards him. They stared at one another, and his gaze dropped to her lips. He wondered what it might be like to kiss her. At that moment, her lips parted, and she stared at him more intensely than ever. He considered making a move. One small step towards her and they'd be standing an inch or two apart. It was a moment locked in doubt and uncertainty. He was sure of his feelings, but not completely sure of hers. Blood raced through him, pushing him to make that move.

But he remembered their boundaries. "It's nothing," he replied.

"This isn't *nothing*," she cried, lifting the lids to the pots. "Ooooh!" she squealed. "Clam chowder! You made *this*?"

"With all the freshest ingredients from the bay," he announced proudly.

"It smells amazing. It *looks* amazing." She looked up at him in awe. "You did this, for our anniversary?"

"To thank you for letting me stay here and all."

She stared at him suspiciously. "You're staying here to help me out, and we both walk away with something at the end. You don't need to thank me for that."

"I happen to like cooking—"

"You do?"

He nodded. "But cooking for one isn't much fun and I don't bother too much when it's just me. But, seeing that we have an occasion to mark, and because I didn't think you wanted to risk being seen out, I decided to throw something together for you."

"This is throwing something together?" She waved her hand around at the kitchen.

"Don't worry, I'll clear it all up."

"I'm not worried, not anymore. And thank you, for this. It's very thoughtful of you."

"After our last restaurant meal, I cancelled dinner at Fellini's thinking you wouldn't want to risk another Jenna surprise."

She grinned. "I might have been overly anxious," she admitted. "I'm blown away, Blake." She looked as if she wanted to hug him.

He shrugged. "This time next year we'll be on our way." It was a sobering thought, and she must have thought the same because she suddenly looked sombre. He hadn't intended to dampen the mood so quickly and had been surprised by her reaction. "To us," he said, lifting his glass of wine in an attempt to bolster the mood. "To us, on our one month anniversary."

"To us," she said, clinking her glass with his.

She set down her glass, and told him she needed to freshen up, and she'd be back.

He sipped his wine when she left, and tried to imagine events a year on from now. A year on, they'd have ended this charade, and he would be a richer man. Only, there were some days when this didn't feel like a charade; but maybe that was just him.

He had already set the table, nothing fancy, nothing overly romantic, no candles, only the cutlery and dishes, sourdough bread and a nice green salad. When she returned, he served the food. They ate, and talked, and laughed about this occasion and commented on the passing of time. He was eager to know how her lunch with her ever-inquisitive friend had gone, and she told him. Then she surprised him by suggesting that they attend the movie night opening together.

"Together?" he echoed, deliberately exaggerating the question.

"You and me, as a couple," she stated.

This was intriguing. Obviously talking to Jenna had convinced her to change her mind.

"Are you sure you're ready for that? If I remember correctly, I'd already suggested this, and it was you who hated the idea. Won't you hyperventilate if someone else sees us?"

She laughed. "I wasn't that bad, was I?" she asked, pushing up her glasses.

"What changed?" She had let her hair down he noticed. It looked so soft and silky that he was tempted to run his hands through it. But it was only a thought and one which he would never act on.

"Jenna knows and maybe it's easier to make out that we're together?" She let out a little groan. "It's difficult to know how to be. I'm not sure I want to spend the whole year lying to Francine."

"We're going to have to lie no matter what. Whether we tell them we're together or not, it's still a lie unless we tell them the *real* truth, and neither of us are going to do that."

She seemed to consider his words. "Let's arrive together."

"And no public displays of affection. No hold hands, let's keep it vague," he suggested.

"Okay." Her lips pulled together into a smile. "Jenna said she was amazed that I hadn't noticed you before. She wanted to know how we got together."

"Whoa…" he said, putting out his hand as if to halt the conversation. "Back up, backup there a second, what did Jenna say?"

"Are you deliberately fishing for compliments?"

"I don't often get them, so, yes, I am." He lifted his wine glass to his lips. "Tell me again what Jenna said."

"Do you have your eyes on Jenna?" she asked with a frown. The tone of her voice suggested that she was playing with him.

"Jenna? No, of course not. She's with Reed." He set down his glass.

"But if she wasn't?"

He blinked. "Still no. She's not the type of woman I'd be interested in."

"What type of woman would you be interested in?"

Her question momentarily disarmed him. How was he supposed to answer that? He looked back at the woman he was interested in and lied. "It's not something I think about given the problems at work that I need to fix. So, tell me. What did Jenna say?"

"You *are* fishing for compliments. I'll set your mind at ease. She said she was surprised that I hadn't noticed you before."

"She's a great girl. I like her already."

Shay smiled. "She was accusing me of being fixated on Rourke and blamed it on that. She said that was the reason I hadn't noticed you."

"What?"

"Rourke, I always thought he was cute." She poured some more wine into their glasses.

"Rourke?"

"Reed's friend. The realtor guy."

"I know who he is." It was as if a ball of lead had dropped into his stomach and was weighing him down.

"You must have seen him at the town hall meetings. He's usually there."

He choked out a laugh. "And you'd know this because you've been keeping a track of his attendance?"

"I'm not *that* bad." She looked contemplative for a moment. "He's very …"

"Very?"

"Charming. He has that debonair air about him."

Yeah? And what did she think of him, he wondered? Her talking about Rourke like that stung like a thorn. He had known the exact length of time that he'd seen Shay at the meetings, and all that time she hadn't even noticed him. She'd had her sights set on someone else. He tried to breathe in, tried to overlook it. "I know him, not as well as I know Reed, but he seems like a good guy."

"He is a good guy. I've had meetings with him, when I've placed some people at his firm."

He recalled that Jenna had said something about Rourke when Blake had unexpectedly walked in on her and Shay.

She'd set her sights on Rourke Halloran.

What an idiot he'd been, thinking that Shay might have changed her feelings for him? That she might have started to feel something for him.

He felt as if he'd been knifed in the ribs. It was Rourke she'd sought out at the town hall meetings. He tried to keep calm, tried to maintain his composure. That last meeting at the town hall, when he'd waited for her at the end, when she'd been talking to Reed and his friends, and she'd come over to him looking annoyed; it all made such perfect sense now as to why she'd been eager for him to leave.

And then he remembered something the guys had mentioned. "Isn't he with someone now?"

"Yes he is."

Was that a sigh he heard escaping from her lips? She sounded disappointed. He stabbed his food with his fork. "If Rourke had been single, would you have asked him?"

"Asked him what?"

"To marry you."

She laughed, completely ignorant of his change in mood. "He's with someone now.

"I heard. But if he wasn't, would you have asked him?"

She set down her fork and looked at him, her expression searching. "I don't know. No. Probably not."

"But if he was available, he would have been your first choice before me, to marry, no?"

A frown line appeared between her brows. "He wasn't a consideration. It was down to you and Rufus Wilson from work."

She wasn't being truthful. "But if he had been single, would you have considered him?" Why wasn't she giving him a proper answer? It seemed as if she was deliberately avoiding the question.

"I... I..." She seemed to be exasperated.

"It's a simple yes or no, Shay."

"No. Because we do business with him. We supply him with suitable candidates."

"Which you also do for Kennedy Tiles." He tried to swallow his food, except it wouldn't go down. The delicious meal he had only just cooked had lost all flavour and taste for him.

"What is this, Blake?" she asked, irritation dancing in her eyes.

"We're having a conversation, that's all. You're obviously attracted to Rourke—"

"I am not attracted to Rourke. Yes, I found him gorgeous to look and an occasional flirt but he's not someone who would notice me."

"And if he had?"

"He hasn't, and he didn't." She'd raised her voice and now sat back looking slightly weary. "Look, there are some guys who are great to have as a fantasy crush—"

"A fantasy crush?"

She covered her face with her hands. "I can't believe we're having this conversation."

"It's enlightening."

"It's uncomfortable. This is the type of conversation I'd have with Jenna, not with someone like you."

"Someone like me? What does that mean?"

Something shifted in those dark eyes of hers, but he couldn't guess at what it was. She seemed a little sad. "A friend. You're a good friend, Blake."

Nothing more? He wanted to ask, but decided against it. He wasn't ready to accept her answer.

"To us," she said, raising her glass midway through their meal. "And to this wonderful dinner you've cooked."

"You've already made a toast," he reminded her.

"I want to make another one."

It took him a moment to lift his glass, because his heart wasn't in it. Because his heart was still recovering from the new revelations that told him she didn't see him the way he saw her.

She smiled at him, but unlike other times, this wasn't a full-watt smile.

He didn't know Rourke too well, but he knew enough about him, and had heard plenty of little comments between the Reed and his friends which suggested that Rourke was a philanderer.

Was that the kind of man Shay was interested in? It didn't matter because she had never been interested in him. All those years of meetings, and she'd had her eyes on Rourke. This was what he had to take note of, and what he'd lost sight of. Living together had altered their relationship but not in the way he'd hoped.

They finished the rest of the meal in silence. He forced himself to eat, not wanting to waste the food even though his appetite had vanished. At the end she thanked him once more. "This has been such a lovely meal. I don't want to get up."

"You don't need to get up," he said, getting ready to rise. "I've made desert."

"There's dessert too?"

"There's always dessert." He forced a smile as he started to clear away the dishes.

She got up. "Let me help you."

So, he let her. "We make a good team," she said, picking up the dirty dishes and walking into the kitchen.

Did they? He suddenly wasn't so sure.

CHAPTER 29

She had taken Jenna's advice and worn her rose-colored dress, the one with the cap sleeves and the skinny, long zipper at the back. The one that fit like a second skin, and showed off her curves, and she'd also let her hair down and put in her contact lenses.

After struggling for a while with the zipper at the back and failing to pull it all the way up, she came out of her bedroom feeling exasperated. Blake was pacing around in the living room looking heart-stoppingly handsome.

She stopped and stared, and then he stopped and stared back.

"You look…" He shook his head, and it made her stomach do a somersault because he didn't need to say anything further. She could tell by the look on his face that she looked good. The mirror had already told her, but the confirmation on Blake's face was priceless.

He was wearing a new suit, something sharper, slicker, and more expensive looking. Goosebumps rippled all over her skin and she suddenly felt light headed. "And you look even smarter than you did on our wedding day," she told him.

He made a noise, as if surprised by her choice of words.

172

"Black suits you," she continued, and moved towards him. She was already excited by the prospect of stepping out with him tonight. She hadn't even considered forewarning Francine, who was sure to be there. She and Blake were going together, but they weren't going to walk around holding hands. Did she even need to say anything to her boss? "Could you do up my zipper?" she asked, and turned around so that she had her back to him. She lifted her hair and moved it to the side. He cleared his throat, and she sensed his hesitation. "I couldn't get to it," she explained.

His fingers gently settled on the zipper, brushing lightly against her skin at the top after he had zipped her up. She shuddered. His touch was soft and gentle, like the fluttering wings of a butterfly skimming along her bare skin, and his hand stayed on her for a few seconds longer after he had finished zipping her up.

She turned around slowly, and stared up at him. "Thank you." But she stayed put, not wanting to move away. He didn't say a word, and it was odd, because he was the one who usually broke the ice, the one who had something to say.

She looked at his lips, as the scent of his aftershave clung to the two-inch empty gap between them. Why did this man never make a move? Did he really never feel anything? Could he not sense this insane zap of electricity that sizzled between them?

A kiss.

Even a light touch of his lips was all she hungered for. Right now, in this heady, magical moment, it seemed like the only logical thing to do.

His grey eyes pierced into her, making her nerves vibrate with joy. Only, Blake didn't move a muscle, just like he hadn't even after their marriage ceremony, and she was the one who'd made the move and kissed him.

This moment was loaded with all the right things—his scent, her perfume, his touch on her skin. What was he waiting for?

Her eyes had been opened. She had been a complete blind dufus to have never noticed just how gorgeous this man was and, more than that, how wonderful he was.

She longed to taste those lips, to feel his hands around her.

He lowered his head, and her heart rate skyrocketed. "We should go," he whispered, his low husky voice causing a heat surge inside her. And then he stepped away. It happened so fast, the ending she hadn't expected to a moment she regularly dreamed of, that she was stunned into silence.

He felt nothing for her.

"Don't forget your clutch bag," he reminded her, as she walked to the door in disappointment. "Or your keys."

She put his change of mood down to work. He'd mentioned lately that he had a lot going on. She reached for his hand as they left the apartment.

"We're putting on a show already?" he asked, giving her a questioning look.

"You don't know who might be watching."

He didn't laugh, but slid his hand into hers.

He wasn't a jealous man, ordinarily, but watching Shay talking to Reed and his friends, especially with Rourke, made him feel uneasy.

He'd been with them but had excused himself in order to get another drink. He walked around the lush lobby of the movie theater, admiring the thick carpet and the thick blood red drapes. White pillars gave the theater an elegance that harked back to earlier times. Old style black and white movie pictures hung on the walls, while on others were colored pictures of the new superheroes and famous actors and actresses from recent years.

The doors to the actual screening rooms were open for guests to go in and admire the plush velvet seats, large and spacious with tiny tables in between them. Coming to the Knight Movie Theater was an experience, Reed had just said, as he'd explained the thinking behind having a pizzeria and an ice-cream parlor inside the cinema, and allowing movie-goers to take in their food and drink and eat them at the tiny tables next to their seats, as they watched a film.

A ticket to the movies here wasn't going to be cheap, but it would be well worth it, Reed had told them.

Reed had done remarkably well with restoring this building it to its former glory. He'd added touches of modern décor which worked surprisingly well with the old style influences. Painted in white outside, Blake was certain that the new movie theater would become one of Starling Bay's new landmarks.

He walked down the aisles of one of the screening rooms, wanting to get away from the crowd that was mostly in the lobby area, still enjoying the free-flowing champagne and canapes. He needed to get away from everyone and everything, but stopped when he saw a woman sitting a few rows in front.

It was Shay's boss.

He tried to turn around and leave, but she'd already seen him. "I was enjoying the quiet," she said, as if she needed to explain.

"Me too," he said, coming to a stop by her row. He wasn't sure what else to say. He and Shay had walked in together, but not holding hands, and now he wasn't sure what Shay had told her. Soon enough things were going to come to a head. Jenna knew they were together, while Francine didn't, at least, this was what he assumed. Something was going to give at some point. "Beautiful building, isn't it?"

"Stunning," she agreed, the enthusiasm in her voice obvious. "I could happily sit here and stare at the blank screen all day." The room was quiet, and the atmosphere reminded him of that of a church. "Who are you hiding from?" she asked.

He laughed. "Nobody."

It was hard to tell if she believed him or not. "Where's Shay?" she asked.

"Talking to her friends," he replied, and then, because he was eager to leave, "I'll let you enjoy more of that peace and quiet before someone else comes along and disturbs you."

"There's no need to leave on my account."

"I'm going to get some food before it runs out," he told her, then smiled and left.

When he stepped back out into the main lobby, Shay in her rose-colored dress was the first person he saw. And then noticed that she and Jenna were talking to Rourke.

Watching them, he wondered where the heck Reed had gone, and where Rourke's current flavor of the month was.

He remained where he was, making no move to go up to them. This night could have been different, it could have been fantastic, what with Shay suggesting that they attend this event together. But ever since he'd discovered her feelings for Rourke, things had changed.

Shay was never going to admit to her feelings for Rourke, and Blake had to read between the lines and come to his own conclusion, and the scene playing out in front of his eyes was more than enough proof.

He had to stop imagining things that were never going to be. Some days, he almost made himself believe that Shay was changing her mind about him, that her feelings were slowly changing, like earlier today when she'd asked him to do up her zipper. She'd turned around and stared at him expectantly. He'd have kissed her if he hadn't had the spectre of Rourke hanging over him.

He could see Rourke had come here with his girlfriend. Shay could see that, too. But every smile, every little trickle of laughter that came from Shay's mouth now made him read a thousand different things into everything.

This wasn't good.

It wasn't who he was.

He wasn't ordinarily a jealous man, but this situation was making him jealous, and he needed to be careful and protect his feelings. And the fact that he was feeling these negative emotions told him that he had let his feelings for Shay get in the way of the arrangement. He had agreed to help her because she seemed to be in trouble, or maybe he'd told himself that lie. As far as he could detect, she didn't seem to be in any trouble. She never spoke about any financial problems. She was close to her parents and tried to see them most weekends, but other than that, she looked to be doing just fine.

Maybe she wanted the inheritance because who wouldn't if they were given the chance?

The question was, did he need the money that badly? Was it worth it, to put up with this for a year, to live with a woman he could never have, and watch her set her heart on a man she couldn't have. *Yet*, he reminded himself. Given Rourke's reputation, maybe Shay was just waiting for one lucky moment when the guy would be single and she'd have the courage to do something about it.

This was a business arrangement, nothing more, and it was his fault for reading more into the situation than there was. He was the one who had misinterpreted things, not Shay, and for that reason he couldn't blame her. But he could keep his distance, as hard as that was going to be.

And yet he found it almost impossible to take his eyes off her. She looked gorgeous. Every time he looked at her she seemed more attractive. It was a wretched predicament to be in. It was just a matter of time before Rourke noticed that Shay was interested.

Where would that leave him?

"Nice evening." He turned to find that Reed had joined him.

He nodded. "You've completely revamped this place. Congratulations."

"Thank you."

The guy had an eye for seeing opportunities and making the most of them. He also had a ton of money to help him. "I'm seriously impressed."

"This place was a part of my childhood. It was a shame when it closed down for so many years. I had to do something to revive it."

"I love the old-style glamor, and the touch of the new. You've made this into Starling Bay's new landmark."

"I certainly hope so."

They stood quietly for a moment, and Rourke, Jenna and Shay were still talking in their group not too far away. He considered that Reed might think it odd that he hadn't joined them. And that was another thing about his and Shay's arrangement, he wasn't sure what people knew. People talked and rumors would fly around faster than one of Hyacinth Fitzsimmons' monthly meeting announcements.

"Great canapes," he stated. "You upped the bar on that, as well."

"A custom order from Fellini's," replied Reed.

"You can never go wrong with Fellini's."

"Come and join us," Reed said, starting to move away. He nodded at the group where Shay was.

"I will. I… uh… I need to get some more of those langoustine canapes."

"You know where we are."

"Join you shortly." He walked towards the buffet tables, took a small plate and helped himself. This wasn't like him, being this miserable, loner-type. He liked to mingle with people, but tonight, he wanted nothing of the sort. He hoped this feeling would soon pass, and he hankered for a return to the pre-wedding days, when Shay had been someone he was interested in talking to, and nothing more. When the town hall meetings were a painless networking opportunity, and when his thoughts were focused more on his business, instead of the shifting sands of his feelings for Shay.

He had to remember that his business was important, and nothing else mattered.

"Eating without me?" It was Shay's voice behind him.

"You looked busy," he said, turning to her.

"We were talking." She patted his arm gently, a move that took him by surprise. They didn't make any public displays of affection, and especially not in front of friends and work colleagues. "You should have joined us."

"I was hungry, and these things are amazing."

"Then you should have told me. I'd have come with you." She squeezed his arm, confusing him further.

"What are you doing?" he asked.

"Just…" Her arm slowly fell to her side.

"You never dictated how we were supposed to be tonight, here," he said, the accusation rising in his throat like bile. Where they supposed to behave as if they were friends, or as if they were an item? What was it to be?

"Dictated?" she asked, letting out an exasperated gasp; something between a breath escaping, and disbelief.

"You're the one who usually decides how we're to be, aren't you?" He lowered his head, but didn't go so far as to whisper in her ear this time. "This is a game, isn't it? What we're doing?"

The light in her eyes died out, like a flame he'd just extinguished.

"Blake Kennedy." Long slim fingers with blood-red nails slid over the lapels of his jacket. "Hello, you."

"Callie?" He looked up. It was just as well that he hadn't taken a bite of his canapes because he would have choked. His ex-girlfriend was back in town, and she looked as gorgeous as he remembered. "This isn't your usual type of event. What are you doing here?" she asked.

He could see Shay looking speechless, and confused. She'd stepped back, or, more like it, Callie had pushed her way in.

"I'm attending the opening of the movie theater, what does it look like?" he shot back. He hadn't seen her in a while. Her job as a freelance project manager took her away to client sites in other states, and that had been part of the problem. They never got to spend much time together. The other part had been her possessiveness. The way he now felt about Shay and Rourke, reminded him of the type of person he didn't want to be.

"I'm back," she told him.

"For how long?" he asked.

She pulled a canape from his plate, and took his napkin. "For a year at least." She took a bite and assessed him, as if she was waiting to see what he made of that news.

Shay cleared her throat. "I think you pushed past me," she said, as Callie turned to look at her, as if she'd only just noticed.

"Did I?" Callie asked, her voice spiking in surprise.

"Yes," Shay replied. "You did." Something told him the two women didn't exactly warm towards one another.

"This is a … friend of mine," Blake said slowly. Shay's face dropped, and this time she swiped a canape off his plate. "Let me know when you're ready to leave," she said to him, before turning on her heel and leaving.

Blake stared at her, the corners of his lips lifting upwards. She was jealous.

"Are you together?" Callie asked.

He hesitated before answering the question. Why had Shay made such a pointed comment before leaving?

"We arrived here at the same time," he replied, knowing that this answer most likely brought up even more questions.

"Oh?" Callie stepped closer to him. "Who is she? She seemed… annoyed."

How should he answer that? He wanted to follow Shay and ask her, but she had returned to Reed and his friends. Her safe haven. So he stayed where he was, and took a step back, because his ex seemed determined to pin herself to him.

"She's from the local recruitment company."

"And are you together?" Callie asked, again.

He didn't want to answer that, because he didn't want to give Callie hope, and the way she was eyeballing him right now, it seemed that 'No', would have been the answer she wanted. He said nothing, because he was tired of telling white lies, and tonight he was especially fed up with keeping up the façade.

Callie swiped another canape off his plate, irritating him so much that he handed over his entire plate to her. "You have it. I've lost my appetite. Excuse me."

He left her and walked past Shay and her friends, over to another group of people he recognized.

For the rest of the evening, he successfully managed to dodge Callie while keeping his distance from Shay. It was awkward, and silly, and yet, there was no way back to one another, not here, not tonight.

The drive home later was quiet, and when they returned home —to her apartment, he reminded himself, not home—there was more silence.

They went their separate ways. She disappeared into her bedroom while he tossed and turned on the couch all night long. The next morning, they managed a 'good morning,' and she still made him his cup of coffee.

"Thanks," he replied, though his voice sounded rougher than he'd intended. Her lips, closed and pressed tightly together, lifted at the corners slightly, in acknowledgement. He gulped his coffee down quickly, wanting to leave because the atmosphere was still tense, despite the outward pretenses of normality. It reminded him of how things had been with Callie towards the end, how little irritations snowballed and became bigger than they were, how he hated the sullenness and miscommunications; how the caring stopped, and the need to be alone became greater than the need to be together.

He hadn't ever thought he would feel like this with Shay, but things were starting to become like that and it had happened quickly. Odd, how a small thing could change everything.

She isn't even with Rourke, he reminded himself, *but she never noticed you,* a small voice inside him said.

Doubt had set in, and now the vines of jealousy curled and crept around his mind, spreading their own poison. He was logical and practical—much like Shay, he'd often thought—preferring to see things in black and white most of the time. It was easier that way, easier to focus on the things that mattered, like his business and his employees. He didn't like being like this, consumed by thoughts and feelings to the detriment of his day-to-day life.

Maybe their sweet and innocent honeymoon period had come to a crashing halt. This was real life, and he couldn't put up with this for another eleven months.

"Gotta go." He set down his half-empty coffee cup, and grabbed his car keys, not wanting to think about the glaring problem staring him in the face. "Have a good day."

CHAPTER 30

She didn't like the atmosphere. What had happened to the easy-going Blake? He had a face like thunder, and she couldn't work out why. What she did know was that the appearance of his ex-girlfriend had changed things.

Did Blake want to get back with her? He seemed surprised to see her, surprised to discover that she was back in town. Worse, he'd seemed reluctant to introduce Shay, and had introduced her as a friend.

Even though they had arrived at the event together, they hadn't announced they were together and they hadn't arrived holding hands or anything. They hadn't fully defined what type of 'relationship' they were going to announce to friends and family. Their initial plan to keep it strictly a secret had been thwarted when Jenna found out, and even though she'd sworn Jenna to secrecy, she wasn't sure how much Reed would have believed it, especially if their behavior at the movie theater opening had been anything to go by. They'd barely spent much time together and Blake had stayed away from her for most of the evening. It made her wonder if Blake had known beforehand that Callie was going to be there.

When she had suggested that they attend the event together, she hadn't been sure herself in what capacity it would be. Their marriage had introduced complications she hadn't been prepared for. Perhaps she had been naïve in thinking she could keep up with the lies, but she was beginning to find that it was draining.

But something had changed between them arriving at the movie theater, and leaving to go home, and she was convinced that it had to be something to do with his ex.

Up until her arrival, Shay had been swaddled in happiness, with her feelings for Blake lately turning into something beyond friendship. Every time he did something for her, shopped for groceries, cooked dinner, caught a spider, made her think he cared. And the anniversary celebration had truly opened her eyes to him.

Francine walked in with an odd smile on her face. "Are you dating Blake Kennedy?"

Shay stopped breathing for a moment, dread seizing up her insides.

"I'll take that as a *yes*." Francine's almost-smile turned full-watt.

"We're friends."

Francine tilted her head, as if she wasn't sure whether to believe that. "Friends?" she murmured.

"He's nice, and we've been getting along a lot better. There's nothing like a choking incident to cement a friendship."

"A friendship?" Francine asked, with a nod of her head. She still looked as if she didn't believe her.

"Yes. Why?" She tried to look blasé about this line of questioning, pushed her glasses up then twiddled with her pencil.

"You're different around one another now," Francine remarked.

"Different, how?"

"Softer."

She laughed. "You were watching us all evening? Because we weren't together for most of the evening." She tried to remember the times during the evening that she and Blake would have been together. Maybe it had been a small mercy that Blake hadn't agreed with her idea to announce to everyone that they were together. Seeing how things had ended she could see it would have been a huge mistake. "And *softer?* What do you mean by that?"

"*You* were different. You *looked* different. That was a beautiful dress, by the way."

"Thank you."

"I haven't seen you make an effort like that for a while."

She laughed again. "What effort?"

"Contact lenses, hair down, figure hugging dress."

"That's Jenna's influence."

"You're still maintaining that you and Blake Kennedy are just friends?"

"We certainly are."

"You make nice friends." Francine raised an eyebrow.

"He's not so bad once you get to know him."

"I can see that about Blake. He's a good looking guy."

She pretended not to hear that.

"He seemed a little … a little….what's the word," said Francine looking around the room as if the perfect word was floating around in the air. "Contemplative," she said, finally.

"What makes you say that?" He'd been fine when they'd arrived at the theater, but he had a face like thunder by the time they left. She was still trying to work out what had happened in between.

"He was in one of the screening rooms, and I was sitting down. He talked briefly but I got the impression he wanted some time to himself. Unfortunately, he found me sitting there."

This was news to Shay, and she wondered if he had heard

something that had dampened his mood, though he'd been more subdued lately, now that she thought about it. She'd been so excited, so happy, and wrapped up in her delusions of love and her feelings for Blake, that she'd missed something.

"I'll ask him, next time I see him," said Shay. Easy enough to say this to Francine, but she knew the reality would be completely different. This morning Blake couldn't get out of her apartment fast enough.

Whatever it was, she was determined that they talked about it, and fixed it. She decided to go home early and fix dinner tonight, something she knew he liked. The way to a man's heart was through his stomach, or so her mother had often quoted. She suddenly remembered that she hadn't called her mom in days, and reached for her phone.

～

"Callie French for you on line two," Nancy announced.

Damn it. She'd called and left messages on his cell phone, and now she was hounding him through his company phone line. "Tell her I'm in a meeting."

"As you wish," said Nancy.

Callie French was an annoyance he could do without.

"Yes!" he barked, when someone knocked on his door. He didn't look up.

"What's upset you now?" asked Ralph, the only employee who could ask him that question when he was in a temper and not get his head bitten off.

"What is it?" he asked impatiently, ignoring the question.

"Nothing." His foreman removed his hat, as he usually did when he was here, and clutched it between both of his hands. "Just wanted to come in and catch up with you."

"I'm catching up with things. Friday is a bad day to come in looking for gossip, Ralph."

"Gossip? You don't gossip," the older man snorted. "I've never gotten anything from you. How was the theater opening? It must have been a fancy event?"

Blake set his pen down, and squeezed the tense pressure points along his eyebrow. "It was."

"Is that all you're giving me?"

"I swear Ralph, sometimes I think you should have been born a woman."

"I'm only asking you. People like me and Nancy don't get invited to these things."

He exhaled slowly. "It was a good night. There were lots of people, and lots of food, and drink. Reed Knight's done that place up really well. You should go, take Nancy, when it opens and they start showing films. Won't be long now."

"She wants to go."

He picked up his pen and was poised to return to work, but Ralph hadn't moved. "Now what?"

"Nothing. Just wondering if Callie French was there."

He threw down his pen. Ralph obviously knew she'd been there. "Is there nothing that Nancy doesn't tell you?"

"She said she's already called you twice this morning."

"Next time she calls I'll get Nancy to re-route the call to the factory floor and you can speak to her instead," Blake growled, and he meant it too. Ralph was familiar with Callie because Blake had complained to him about her during their final break up weeks.

"If you're not interested in her, just give me the sign and I'll arrange a date for you to meet with my niece."

Blake had lost all of his patience completely. "You have three seconds to leave the office, Ralph. You're seriously trying my patience."

"You're like a bear. I'm only trying to cheer you up."

"This isn't cheering me up."

Ralph threw his hands up in the air, as if to gesture that he had tried. "Okay," he said, then left.

What was wrong with people? What was wrong with every interaction in his life? Things were falling apart with him and Shay, and Ralph was being a huge nuisance, and Callie was being an even bigger nuisance.

Thank goodness it was the weekend tomorrow. A second later he was filled with dread at the thought of being at home with Shay. But, he reasoned, she would likely be at her parents' house tomorrow, so at least he'd have the day to himself.

They needed to talk and clear the air, because this sullen silence between them couldn't continue.

When his cell phone rang again, he answered it, even knowing that it was Callie at the other end. He'd been interrupted so many times today, and was in such a bad mood, that speaking to Callie seemed like a tiny distraction.

"I have a proposition for you," was the first thing she said.

"For me?" he replied, determined not to fall for any of her sweet talk.

"Meet me, for a drink, and I'll tell you."

"If this is a ploy to see me, I'm not interested."

"It's not a ploy, Blake, I promise you. It's a suggestion. One drink. Meet me for lunch."

"I can't do lunchtime."

"Tonight?" she suggested.

Tonight? The thought of going home didn't appeal, and meeting Callie seemed a better alternative. Just the fact that he preferred being away from Shay, told him everything he needed to know about their current living situation. "I can do tonight."

"Great. Tonight then. Seven o'clock at the Blue Velvet Bar."

He hung up, not even caring whether this was a lure to get him to meet with her.

He met her later as planned, but his heart dipped a little as soon as he saw her and he questioned what he was doing there, and why he hadn't canceled. Seeing her instead of Shay, sent pangs of guilt shooting through him. This didn't feel right.

"You came," gushed Callie, standing up as he walked towards her. Throwing her arms around him, she hugged him tight, pressing her body against his, as if they were familiar again. He sprang back, moving away from her in a heartbeat, already feeling as if he'd cheated—even though technically this wasn't cheating. Even if he and Shay had been married, this wouldn't be classed as cheating, yet it felt like it.

All of a sudden he wanted to be back in Shay's apartment. It was her he needed to talk to, not Callie, and he didn't even care about her proposition.

"I ordered you a drink." She sat down and he sat across the table from her. "Bourbon on the rocks, just what you like at the end of the week." She smiled.

He wasn't surprised that she had remembered, or that she was telling him that she had remembered. He knew Callie. She wanted something. But he wasn't interested in getting back with her, if that's what she had in mind. "What's the proposition?" he asked, eager to hear it anyway.

"You're going to be three staff down come Christmas," she announced. He banged down his glass and groaned. Why the heck could Nancy not keep her mouth shut? Didn't she know that he and Callie had split up a long time ago?

"Nancy and I got on well, when you and I were dating," she told him, as if she'd read his thoughts."

"You and I split up a while ago, and Nancy should know better than to tell you things that are going on in my company," he growled. He needed to have words with both Ralph and Nancy.

"Ouch, Grouchy," she replied, her red-stained lips spreading into a smile. She looked good. Amazingly good, he thought, taking in her appearance. She was tall and willowy, with long hair, and a heart-shaped face. And her full, luscious lips were hard to miss.

An image of her kissing him suddenly flashed across his eyes, and he shook his head, wanting to forget it. "What's your proposition?"

"My contract here ends in December. I could do the maternity leave cover for you when your office ladies are having their babies."

He laughed. "And you'd do what exactly? You're over qualified."

"It's three women I'd be replacing. You'd only need to take me on, and I'm pretty sure I could do the job of those three women. It's office work," she rolled her eyes. "How hard can it be?"

She had to be kidding him. "You're a project manager," he explained.

"You're thinking about it, aren't you?" she asked, sitting back and staring at him intently. "You're looking mighty fine, Blake." Her gaze lowered to his chest, then back up to his face. "Are you working out more often these days?"

"And what if I am?"

She sat forward. "You never did tell me about your little friend from last night."

"What exactly did you want to know?"

"Are you together?"

When he hesitated, she made a face, a condescending type of are-you-being-serious face. "You *are?*"

"We're friends."

"You and I are friends," Callie said, dropping her voice to a sexy whisper. "And we've been more than friends before."

"And thank goodness that's over." He took another sip of the bourbon, then decided he didn't want anymore.

"That's not a nice thing to say."

"But it's true. We both wanted out towards the end. You can't have forgotten that."

"Time makes things look different," she said, softly.

Time had changed everything. Hindsight had made him see Shay in a different light, and the last few days had cast yet another filter on the way he saw things.

And even though Callie's proposition was so ludicrous that he wasted no further time in considering it, it made him see that as beautiful and as sexy as Callie was tonight, he wasn't interested. And as strained and awkward things were between him and Shay, he much rather preferred to be with Shay, than stay here.

"No," he said, standing up.

"No?"

"No to your proposition. You can't be serious," he challenged. "It would never work."

"I *am* serious. We could both help each other out."

"It's a stupid idea. I don't need you, nor does my company."

"Where are you going?"

"Home."

It wasn't home exactly, and he still had mixed feelings about what it was, and about what he was doing there, but it was better than being here with his ex.

CHAPTER 31

"Are you sure you're alright?" Jenna asked.

"Yes," Shay forced a small laugh, then glanced at the clock. It was way past the time when Blake should have been home.

"You and Blake didn't look as lovey as I thought you'd be. Especially given the fact that you're living together."

"Shhh," said Shay. "Are you alone?"

"Yes, it's only me here. Reed's meeting his friends. You know how they like to have their boys' nights. We should do our girls' nights, like we used to—before you started your secret life with Blake Kennedy."

Shay made a face then stretched out her legs on the couch. She lay down, assuming the same position that Blake would when he fell asleep here each night. "I don't have a secret life," she lied, and wondered what that day would be like when she and Blake finally made it to the end of the year and claimed their financial rewards. Her life, and that of her parents, would change forever after.

Some days she still couldn't believe it, just like she couldn't believe that she had taken part in the creation of such a complicated and intricate spider's web of lies. She'd unwittingly ensnared Blake into that same web, and now she wondered if he felt trapped. Jenna had called to discuss last night's movie night opening. She'd called her at work a number of times but Shay hadn't been able to talk then.

Francine's earlier observation about her and Blake seeming aloof was further compounded by what Jenna was telling her. There was something going on with Blake and she had missed it entirely.

"I have no idea what's up with him," she confessed. "He was perfectly fine before." And she proceeded to tell her about the surprise dinner that he had made, although she omitted all mention of it being an anniversary dinner.

"I still don't understand exactly what's going on with you two," said Jenna probing. "How much longer is he going to stay at your apartment?"

Shay paused a moment, trying to find an answer that wouldn't later require two more white lies to support it. "The work at his house should be over soon, so..."

"Because your mom and dad will get the shock of their lives if they suddenly turned up at your place."

"Like you did, you mean?"

"It's just as well I did," retorted Jenna. "I still don't think you've told me everything. You're hiding something, Shay."

"I am doing no such thing."

"How is your dad?"

The conversation suddenly turned serious again. "My dad's got a slight temperature."

"Oh no."

"I'm sure it's just a passing thing. He's given us a lot of scares while he's been having the chemo treatments."

"The poor thing."

He hadn't been too well this morning, her mother had said. He was running a temperature and her mother was going to keep an eye on him. When Shay had called an hour ago, the temperature was still high, but not rising. At least she'd get to see them tomorrow. Things were always so much more frightening to hear on the phone.

She turned when she heard the key turn in the lock. "Blake's here," she whispered.

"Good luck. Let's meet on Sunday to talk properly," Jenna said.

"Let's do that." She hung up quickly and had barely had a chance to stand up, when Blake was inside, and staring at her. "Are you ill?"

She sat up and put her feet on the floor. "No. I was on the phone to Jenna. Do I look ill?"

He set down his briefcase slowly. "No. You were lying down, that's all."

"I made dinner."

His brows pushed together.

When he didn't say anything, she said, "I was expecting you home at the normal time. I made you steak."

"Oh."

That didn't sound too enthusiastic. Nothing like her reaction to him the other day when he had cooked the anniversary dinner for her.

She stood up, feeling powerless sitting down. Tension crackled in the air and she folded her arms bracing herself for something, but she didn't know what. "How come you're so late?"

"That sounds like the sort of question a wife would ask a husband," he said, but his voice didn't sound soft, or normal, and she wasn't sure how to take his comment.

It dawned on her that he'd probably gone out for dinner or met a friend, though in the time that they had been together, this had happened only once and he'd called and told her. "You could have called," she said. "I waited for you, and I didn't think you'd eat. I haven't eaten."

"Me neither. I went for a drink."

As this was sinking in, he added, "With Callie. You met her last—"

"Your ex-girlfriend?" Something sharp and twisted jabbed at her heart, and made it sink to the base of her stomach. He'd gone to see his ex-girlfriend?

"She called me," he said, loosening his tie before removing it.

"She called you?"

She watched as he removed his blazer. She only noticed it now, that he probably did this daily but she was in her bedroom or in the kitchen, and didn't see that he had nowhere to put his clothes, and that he usually got changed in the bathroom into his casual clothes, and put away his work clothes.

A month of this would be enough to drain anyone.

This wasn't easy for him.

And he looked weary today.

The appearance of his ex probably made him see the life he'd given up; in order to help her, a woman he didn't even know as a close friend, and he'd done this for her.

Maybe he'd had enough.

It would explain the sudden change in his mood and personality.

"Are you… are you…" A lump mushroomed in her throat and held there. His confession had speared her in half, and she didn't know how to react, how to save face, how to appear strong. "Are you fed up, Blake?"

"Fed up?" he echoed, taking a deep breath which was more frank and honest than his words.

"I'm sorry I made you do this," she said. Taking the blame

would stop her from focusing on the hurt and betrayal—him meeting Callie certainly felt like betrayal, even if it wasn't.

"It was a mutual decision. You didn't force me," he replied.

He might have gone into it thinking he could do this, and the promise of so much money at the end would have been enough to make up most people's minds, but the day-to-day life, and living with someone you had no feelings for, that was harder to pretend. "But neither of us knew what we were getting ourselves in to," she said softly.

He raked his hands through his hair. "That's true. I didn't expect it would be this difficult, especially when… when..." Her ears pricked up, anticipating the truth she felt sure he was about to divulge. "When your heart is elsewhere."

She would have stumbled and fallen back onto the couch, if she hadn't forced herself to stand tall. "Is that why you've been distant?"

"Things are different, and … this isn't an easy situation to be in, is it, Shay? Living the way we do."

So it was true. He wanted to get back with Callie. She wanted to fall to the couch and curl up and try and comfort herself. "I never expected it to be easy, and I was surprised at just how easy it was, until…until yesterday."

He frowned as they stood across the living room, looking at one another. "I can't be second best," he said, confusing her.

Second best? To whom? She wanted to ask him what he'd told Callie of their arrangement, but then she remembered that he'd introduced her as his friend the other night.

"You shouldn't have to be second best. You're a great guy." There was so much she wanted to say to him, and about how good he was, and how much she appreciated him and valued him being around.

How she was starting to fall in love with him.

"Admit it," he said, taking a step towards her. "You feel

trapped.”

“Me? Trapped?”

“I’ve been out this evening with Callie, and that’s not right. That’s not what a husband would do, but at the same time, we’re not husband and wife. Where does that leave you? Where does that leave me?”

She swallowed, and tried to summon all the willpower in her body to remain strong. “It’s only a fake marriage, Blake. It’s not like we have any feelings for one another. My equation. That’s all I think of to get through each day. It helps.”

“It doesn’t help me,” he growled, his quiet rage surprising her.

The facades people put up surprised her. They could fool anyone. People were so good at hiding their true feelings. She had believed that they’d reached another level in their relationship, and she felt sure he’d felt the same way, but looking back now, that was all a mirage. It wasn’t real. She’d been so desperate for him to feel something for her that she hadn’t seen what was in front of her face. Blake was only fulfilling the deal. It was she who was getting carried away with crazy love-struck dreams.

“We never talked about what we’d do if there were other people,” she said, waiting for his reaction.

“We didn’t discuss much beyond saying we’d take it a day at a time, and well, here we are.”

No wonder he felt trapped if he wanted to reignite things with Callie. “And then I tell myself that the money is worth it, but I ask myself if that’s really true. Is the lure of half a million dollars’ worth feeling like this?”

“Feeling like how?” She held herself together, tightening her arms and clenching all the muscles in her body. She couldn’t be soft, couldn’t let him see that she was ready to crumple into a heap at his words. She didn’t want to hear how he felt. Didn’t want to hear about Callie. Didn’t want the trauma of accepting that she meant nothing.

Money wasn't important. She'd gone into this deal thinking it would help, but she never expected to fall for him.

But the money is important.

Her equation kicked in.

The money was life-changing, and to her father it could be life-saving. She couldn't afford to back out of this now. She *had* to make this work, and they had to get through the next eleven months—long and painful months—and then be done with. It was too much to think about now. "We should talk about this tomorrow, or soon," she said, remembering that she was going to see her parents. "We can come to some sort of arrangement."

"Arrangement?" he asked, quietly. "Shay, I'm not that kind of guy. I don't know if I can be here, and pretend not to be. It's hard enough as it is."

"But the money," she said quietly. Her father needed that money. "Think of what it could do for you."

He looked at her with narrowed eyes. "It's always been about the money for you, hasn't it?"

"Always. Wasn't it about the money for you?" It killed her to say it, but she had to.

He didn't answer and instead seemed angry about something. If anyone should have been angry it was her. She'd cooked dinner and he hadn't shown any signs of wanting to eat. While she'd been hoping for a proper conversation, in order to find what had made him so grumpy, she hadn't expected *this*.

Things had gone from fairly calm to explosive in a matter of moments.

He slipped on his jacket again. "I'm going to sleep at my place tonight," he said, picking up his briefcase. "We could both do with having some space."

She opened her mouth to protest, but knew it would be futile, so instead she said, "Okay."

CHAPTER 32

It surprised her, how calm she felt throwing away his steak. She ate her dinner after Blake left, and that surprised her too; that she had an appetite.

And then she went to bed, alone in her apartment for the first time in over a month.

She put it down to her logical side taking over, and all the emotional heart-breaking turmoil pushed away out of sight. She couldn't think about Callie or Blake, and their future plans, and what he was going to do about the inheritance.

She would put it out of her mind and think about it after she had visited her parents.

But when her mother called her early in the morning, waking her up when it was still dark outside, crying and telling her that her dad's temperature had spiked and that he was back in the hospital, she shot out of bed and drove straight to the hospital.

Her mother's bloodshot eyes, and wrinkled expression were the first things she saw as she flew through the doors and into the hospital waiting room.

"Where is he?" Shay asked, her heart thumping in her throat. She hated hospitals. The more she had to visit them, the more her hatred grew, even though these places which evoked such bittersweet emotions had so far kept her father alive.

"The doctors are tending to him. You came so quickly, sweetie."

"I couldn't sleep. I had to come." She grabbed her mother's hand. "He's going to be fine, mom. This is normal." The nausea and fatigue and vomiting were normal, as was the hair loss, but she thought this second round of chemo had gone well. The temperature spiking worried her. She always dreaded that her father's immune system was so weak, that he wouldn't be able to fight off any more infection.

Whatever the best money can buy, she reminded herself. Though she wouldn't be in a position to pay for everything this year. In a few months' time she'd run out of the money she had borrowed and would need to raise or get some more.

Hang in there, dad, she prayed.

They had been told to stay away from her father, in order to let him recover, and to lessen the chance of infection, especially now while they were trying to make his temperature go down. Shay and her mother stayed in the waiting room for the entire day, only getting up to eat, or take a walk or use the washroom.

They went home in the evening, and returned on Sunday, and by Sunday afternoon, her dad showed signs of improving. They sat by his bedside, and waited. He opened his eyes every now and then and muster a weak smile, and they would tell him to rest, to get better, and to talk later.

"Shouldn't you be getting back?" her mother asked on Sunday evening.

"I told Francine I was going to stay here for a few days."

"You don't need to, sweetie. You don't want to take liberties, especially since your boss has been so good to you."

"She understands, Mom. She knows I need to be here."

She had called Jenna and told her in the morning that she

wouldn't be able to make their Sunday get together, then updated her about her father's condition.

"It sounds like he's getting better," said Jenna, when Shay called her a little while ago to tell her that her father's temperature had gone down. "Your dad likes to scare everyone, doesn't he?"

She looked through the window at his sleeping face and smiled. "He'd given me a real scare this time." This was only the second chemo cycle. He had another two to go and she and her mother were going to be worried sick until he was finished with all of them and was in remission. That was months down the line yet.

"When are you coming back?" Jenna asked.

It was the first time she'd considered that question. She didn't know, and Francine hadn't pressed for a date for her to return. "Maybe a few more days. Once dad's home and settled."

"Call me if you need anything."

Her mother was starting to fall asleep at her dad's bedside. Shay sent her home early, and told her that she would stay by her father's side until the end of visiting hours. She planned to do the same for the next few days, only letting her mom come for short intervals because her mom needed her energy and rest, because once Shay returned to work, her mom would need to be on full alert caring for her dad.

Money. She was doing it solely for the money.

Blake spent Friday night at his place, and reveled in the luxury of having his own bed, and being able to get out of bed wearing only his boxer briefs, and walk around his house wearing nothing but that.

It was freedom!

Yet late on Saturday, he returned to Shay's apartment out of a sense of duty, and of wanting to keep his side of the deal, and because he'd had time to think and calm down.

Callie's reappearance in his life had upset things, and stoked his anger.

In his rage, he'd completely forgotten that Shay had cooked for him, and she'd waited for him, and then he'd turned up and they'd had the kind of simmering disagreement that they'd never had before.

He'd felt terrible about the dinner and had returned on Saturday hoping to make it up to her. They hadn't really had a proper conversation on Friday. They'd thrown thinly concealed angry comments at one another, even though they were sensible, rational people who should have been able to talk things through properly.

But affairs of the heart weren't sensible, rational things. With Callie in the mix, it didn't surprise him that this had brought out the worst in him.

But on finding the apartment empty, he felt disappointed. Shay was most likely with her parents, so he didn't contact her. But when by late evening on Sunday, Shay still hadn't arrived; he called her only to find her phone on voicemail.

A few hours before midnight, when she still wasn't at home, he became more worried and left her a few messages on her phone.

And when, on waking up on Monday morning, she hadn't replied or called him, he got completely worried.

She could have had an accident, returning home from her parents. His heart lurched; she could have had an accident on Saturday, when he'd assumed she was staying over at her parent's house.

She could be injured, or dying, or ...

He didn't have a number for her parents, but he had the agency's number, and he also had Reed's. Maybe Jenna would know more than Shay's work colleagues? He picked up his phone and called Reed.

After getting Jenna's number, he called her.

"Hi, it's Blake, Shay's … friend. We met the other--"

"I know who you are. Hey, Blake! What's up?"

Her chirpy manner made him feel at ease, because he'd had been hesitant when calling her; only concern for Shay had made him push through. "Shay's not been at home. I'm worried. Have you heard from her?"

"Didn't she call and tell you?"

His gut tightened. "Tell me what?"

"Her dad. He's ill. They rushed him back to the hospital over the weekend when his temperature spiked."

Her dad was ill? How come he was the last to know? "I… I had no idea."

"She really didn't call you?"

"No. I was expecting her back on Saturday night. I've called her many times and left messages."

"She's been by her dad's bedside most of the time. He's better now. She said she's letting her mom get some rest so she's staying with her dad, and doing more of the hospital shift."

"She called you?"

The pause told him 'yes'. "She called to let me know we wouldn't be able to meet yesterday."

"What's wrong with her dad?" Shay clearly didn't want him to know, but he felt it was his business to find out.

Another pause followed.

"You can tell me, Jenna. Shay doesn't always tell me everything." He had no idea what her friend would make of this comment, maybe one day if and when they told her the truth, she'd understand, but right now, he needed to know. "She'd have told me eventually."

"He's… he's got lung cancer. I mean, they've removed it, and he's having chemo, and…"

Lung cancer?

No wonder she was rushing home every weekend.

He stood up taller, ran a hand through his hair, wondering, piecing together the snippets of conversation and her weekend visits home to see if it might bring up any clues.

The money.

The last thing she'd spoken about on Friday when they'd had their disagreement was about money. It was possible that she was helping her parents out with the medical expenses. Maybe.

"Which hospital?"

"Are you going there?" Jenna sounded dubious. "Because if she hasn't told you, I don't think she wants you to know. She might get angry if she finds out I've told you everything."

"You haven't told me everything, Jenna, but I intend to find out. I need to see her, to make sure she's okay."

"You didn't hear it from me."

"I didn't."

He noted down the hospital name, then called work and told Nancy he'd be out for most of the day.

CHAPTER 33

"He's doing well," the doctor told her, when he had finished examining her father and had come out into the waiting room to speak with her. "With any luck, he'll be able to go home in a day or two."

"And the chemo?"

"We won't start the third cycle until he's good and ready. But he's looking much better, and we're pleased with his recovery."

"That's excellent news, Doctor. Thank you."

She walked in to see her dad. He was sitting propped up with pillows, and looked healthier than he had in days. "Dad," she said, smiling, and shaking her head at the same time, as if he was a child. "You scared us."

"I scared myself."

She held his hand. "We just need you to stay strong and get better. Two more chemo cycles, Dad, and then we're home free."

Her dad looked at her with a somber expression. "It's not always that simple. Lung cancer success rates…"

"Are great. *Yours* is going to be great."

"The cost…" he murmured.

She squeezed his hand gently. "Is not a problem. I told you."

"You should go back to work soon. I wouldn't want your boss to fire you."

"Francine would never fire me. She wanted me to tell you that you're in her thoughts and prayers."

"You're a good girl, Shay."

"And you're a good dad, Dad."

She sat like that for a while longer, until her mother came in and told her to take a break. "You look as if you've slept well, Mom," Shay commented. Her mother had gone from looking haggard and sleep deprived to more of her former self.

Shay considered the idea of commuting to work from her parents' place. It wasn't impossible, and it would help her mother a lot. She would think about it later, when she was back at home. She could help her parents out a lot more by staying with them, rather than seeing them at weekends only, at least until her dad's chemo was over. She walked out, thinking how helpful it would be to have the help of private nurses. This time next year, thanks to Great Aunt Dena, she would be able to afford such help.

If only Blake would go along with the ruse.

She was about to walk towards the exit doors to go outside, when she blinked twice. There, sitting in the waiting room, looking at her, was Blake.

Blake?

What was he doing here?

Confused thoughts ran riot through her mind. He stood up and started walking towards her before she'd finished wondering how he'd managed to find her.

"What are you—" But before she could finish her sentence, he put his arms around her and held her. Not too tight, not too loose. Not an acquaintance-like hug, nor a lover's embrace—but somewhere in between. Something that was perfectly in keeping with the in-between nature of who they were to one another.

He didn't let go so quickly. At first it surprised her, but then she allowed herself to sink against him. Allowed her arms to slip around his back. Allowed him to hold her just-a-little-closer.

He pulled away slowly. "You should have told me."

She blinked, because there were so many questions, and she didn't know where to start. "How did you—"

"Jenna told me," he said. "I was worried when you didn't come home on Saturday."

"You came back on Saturday?" She'd got the impression that he had wanted to stay away for longer than a day, that he needed to get away from her, that he was feeling trapped. "Why did you come back so soon?"

He snorted. "Would you have rather I didn't come back at all?"

No. Never. She didn't want to imagine what that would be like, to not have Blake in her life, and at the same time, she didn't want him to feel trapped on account of her. She had been wrestling with this very thing when she'd found out about her father. "Callie," the word flew out of her mouth before she could stop it.

"Callie?" His brows pushed together. "What about her?"

"I thought… I thought that's why you wanted time to yourself. Why you left on Friday."

"Because of her?"

"You met up with her."

He breathed out slowly. "We need to talk, about this, and other things, but none of that is important right now." He took her hand. "I didn't know about your dad, Shay. Why didn't you say anything?"

"It didn't seem right, or important, or any of your business," she replied, truthfully.

He took her other hand, and she liked the feel of his thumbs gently stroking the back of her hand. With her tired and fogged up brain, she was having difficulty understanding why he was doing this, but she didn't think to ask just yet because it felt good. Seeing him felt good. Having him here, holding her the way he had, and now standing here, staring into her eyes, and talking as if the other people in the waiting room were invisible, all of it felt good and helped her to shut out the outside world.

"You didn't think it would help to tell me?"

"Help who?" she asked.

"Help you. I can see now why you went to see your parents every weekend. So much has fallen into place because I now know about your father being ill. But, Shay, so many lies. Our life together is built on them."

Guilt rained down on her. "I know, and I'm sorry. Maybe it would have made sense to tell you at the start. But I wanted it to be your choice—being with me because you stood to gain something—unfettered by the thought that my father's health depended on it." He opened his mouth to protest but she shook her head. She needed for him to hear her out. "I was scared that if I told you, you might feel unable to leave if it got too much. You've slept on a couch for goodness sake, who does that? I need to fix that somehow, get two single beds or something in my room—"

"Hey," he looked as if he was about to touch her face, but his hand dropped back to his side. "Don't worry about any of that. It's not important."

She was determined to explain. After all, who did this? Even for half a million dollars? Who would put their life on partial standby the way he had done, to help her out, a woman who was almost a stranger? "I wanted you to be able to walk away if it all got too much."

"You carried this load all alone."

"We entered an agreement." She lowered her voice, "And I didn't feel it necessary to tell you everything, just the things that mattered."

"Which were?"

"That I was single and that," she stepped closer, "We can't talk about that here," she said, looking around her.

"Then let's go somewhere—"

"Shay." Her head turned to the direction of her mother's voice. She watched her mother's gaze examine her and Blake, and it was too late to move her hands away from his. She knew how this would look, because there was no other way it could look.

"Shay?" Her mother stared at her in disbelief. "*Who* is this?"

Before she could answer, Blake extricated his hand from hers, and faced her mom, then offered his hand. "I'm Blake, Shay's… friend."

"Shay's *friend?*" her mother echoed.

Now she was in a bind. Given how the two of them had been standing, it was obvious that they were something more than friends. She didn't ordinarily hold hands with a guy unless he was her boyfriend. Yet, what were she and Blake? He'd held her hands and hugged her close, but was that a sympathy reaction or something more? Her mother's curious eyes settled on her. "Well?"

"This is…Blake…I was going to tell you sooner or later…"

"Then tell me sooner," her mother requested. "Like, right now."

"He's…ugh…we met at a town hall meeting…and…" She struggled to explain and Blake's thumb sweeping over her hand, and sending a rash of goose bumps up her back wasn't helping. "And he's uh…uh…" When he did it again, she lost the ability to think straight.

"We've been seeing one another for a short while, Ma'am."

Well, that made things a heck of a lot easier. Her mother beamed as if she'd just heard that she'd won an all-expenses paid vacation to an exotic island. "Seeing one another? This is good news, I must say. The very best news I've heard for months!" Her mother looked the happiest Shay had seen her in a while.

"I'm sorry to hear about Mr. Donovan. I hope he's better now?"

"He's on the road to recovery. It's going to take a while, but once he's recovered from this setback, we'll get there, won't we sweetie?" Her mother turned to her. Shay smiled weakly. "Mom, we were just going out for a short walk."

"You go along, sweetie. Don't you worry about me. Go, go," she almost shooed them out of the waiting room.

They were still holding hands as they left the hospital building. Maybe it was the fresh air, or maybe it was having her mother off her back, but she felt a little lighter as they walked along the hospital grounds. It was refreshing, the fresh air on her face and the sun's rays kissing her skin.

She loosened her hand, waiting for Blake to let go but he didn't.

"This is why you need the inheritance, isn't it?" he asked in a voice so soft, she barely heard him.

"Yes."

He tugged at her hand, forcing her to stop walking. Then he pulled her towards him so that they faced one another. "I wish you'd told me, but I understand why you didn't. I hate to think you carried all this worry with you; that you thought you needed to do it all alone."

"It was something I had to do. I don't want my dad to … " She didn't want to think about the worst case scenario, even though there had been countless nights when she'd been unable to sleep because of it. "Everything costs. The tests, the treatment, the x-rays, the blood tests. I've taken out loans and I would have continued to. I still have to because I've run out—"

"You don't have enough to cover the bills?"

"I have enough, but I can see in a few months' time I will

need to take out a bigger loan. But that's my problem to deal with, not yours." She paused, unsure how to say it. "I need you to see this through… this charade of you and me, just to the end of the year."

"Of course. Of course I will. There's no question of me bailing on you. Ever."

"But, you feel trapped."

He looked confused. "No, *you* feel trapped."

"No I don't. Why would you say that?"

"Rourke."

She stared at him in sheer confusion. "Rourke? Reed's friend?"

"I don't know of any other Rourke, do you?"

"What about him?" she asked.

"You like him, don't you?"

"Wh—what are you talking about?"

"The things you've said about him. It's only a matter of time before he comes to his senses, Shay, and notices you."

She shook her head, then wiped her hands over her face, realizing the enormity of his confusion. "I had a crush on him, a girlie, silly, absurd little crush. He's far too flirtatious and charming for my liking. I prefer men who are more grounded, and kind and considerate, and sensitive. Like you."

He lifted an eyebrow as if this was news to him, prompting her to think that she really did need to spell things out to him. "Do you really have no idea?"

"About what?"

He really didn't. "Why did you meet with Callie the other night? You wasted a good steak dinner."

"I apologize for that," he said, turning to walk, and prompting her to follow him because they were still holding hands. "I came back to your apartment on Saturday, when I remembered that you'd made dinner, and I'd barely acknowledged it. I'm sorry."

"It was a good steak. I threw yours away."

"Ouch."

"It's Callie. She brings up all sorts of feelings in me, none of them good," he added hastily much to her relief.

"If that's the case, then why did you meet with her?"

"Because I can't look at you without seeing you and Rourke together."

Her eyes flew wide open in surprise. "Me and him together? He's with someone."

"I know, but he's never with someone for too long, is he? According to Reed, anyway."

"He seems to be particularly besotted by his current girlfriend," she pointed out. At least, this was what Jenna had told her.

"I don't know about that," Blake continued. "When Callie called me with a proposition, I took the easy way out. I met her for the distraction she was, and because I couldn't bear coming home to you in the evening. The past week hasn't exactly been easy."

He was right. They'd been off with one another for a while.

"The movie theater opening night painted another picture for me. And based on stuff from the past, stuff Jenna had said that day I walked in, and what you had said about liking Rourke over the years…what was I supposed to think?"

She recalled the events he mentioned, and could see how he might have gotten the wrong idea. They'd both been living in a situation where they'd had to hide their true feelings for one another. It had been easy enough to see something else, something that wasn't true.

"What do you think?" she asked him, needing to know once and for all. She needed this marriage to work, for a reason that could possibly mean life or death for her father. She didn't want this man whom she had come to care for, to be in a situation he no longer felt comfortable in.

"It's not what I think, Shay," he said, coming to a stop by a bench. They sat down, a few inches apart, and were no longer holding hands. His face turned serious. "It's what I know."

"And what do you know?" she asked, clasping her hands together and resting them over her knees.

"I know that I've always liked you, right back from the start, from the very first town hall meeting I attended."

She didn't even remember the first time she saw him.

"Your spectacles were tight at the back, and they were hurting your ears. It was a new pair, and you kept taking them off and complaining about them."

Goodness.

Her insides flipped as he spoke of something that now seemed so long ago, but which she now remembered. She had a vague recollection of him at that time, but nothing more.

"I remember thinking how nice you were, how friendly and helpful. It was my first time at these events, and you introduced me to the people you knew. And then at every meeting after that, you and I always spoke." His voice was so soft, as if laced with fond memories, as he went back in time.

"That was a long time ago, Blake." He hadn't come to her attention until the Heimlich incident, and now she felt even more guilty.

"I noticed you from then on. Not in a creepy or stalker-ish way, it was just that I always liked talking to you. And then the Heimlich maneuver happened." He couldn't help but smile at that. Come to think of it, neither could she.

"That was an event, wasn't it?" she commented.

He nodded. "And then after that, you asked to meet me, and asked for my help, you told me about your Aunt Dena… I couldn't help but think that of all the people you could have asked for help, you asked me. There was no way I was going to bail on you. You asked me to help you, when before I wasn't even sure you noticed me. But as we got to know one another, things became harder. I found myself liking you even more, and thinking of you, and I couldn't halt the way my feelings ran away with me."

She stared at him, taking in each and every feature and thinking how she often went to sleep thinking of him, and with his face etched firmly in her mind's eye, and how now, she could sit here and just breathe it all in; his expression, his voice, his words.

And now he was opening his heart to her and telling her the things she'd always wanted him to feel for her, but had never really expected that he would.

Except that he did. He had. He was telling her exactly how he felt, and it scared her, the depth of his emotion. It scared her a little, before lifting her up and making her heart swell with happiness. "You have no feelings for your ex?" she asked, needing clarification.

"None."

"And you'd be okay to see this through, until the end?"

"Yes."

Things had changed, and yet neither of them seemed willing to make a move and state how things would be going forward.

Maybe eliminating the threats was enough; losing the lies and forgetting the Callies of this world which cast a shadow over what she and Blake could be to one another. Now was not the time to sit and make plans of how they would be with one another.

For now it was enough that they had talked things out a little, opened their hearts and shared authentically. She was still holding back, not able to freely express her emotions, because these past few days at the hospital had sucked up so much of her life and soul, but Blake's words gave her so much hope.

There were still other things she would keep to herself, for now, like the full explanation of the inheritance. That ridiculously large sum was too big for anyone to make sense of and she was never going to get that, but she felt Blake had a right to know, perhaps after their year was up.

For now, she and Blake had to learn to get to know one another properly.

The rest would come later.

CHAPTER 34

Shay finally returned home on Wednesday evening around dinner time. He hadn't felt right staying in her apartment without her, but she had insisted that he stay there and keep up the pretense.

The pretense.

Only, it wasn't so much a pretense now that he had told her about his feelings. He still wasn't sure about her feelings though, and she planned to fix that once the worry about her father eased off.

Hopefully, getting to the end of the year would be easier for them both now without the lies.

When he heard the key turn in the lock, he rushed to the door, eager to see her. This time, as she stepped through, they hugged and held one another in a way they hadn't been able to at the hospital, often under the watchful eye of her mother.

She unpacked while he made dinner.

They ate together and she told him about her father and how he was so much better and had come home yesterday, and how he would be ready to start chemo in a few weeks' time.

He cleaned up, and refused to let her help him, telling her to go and relax in front of the TV. She didn't look her usual self. Her eyes were dark, and she looked gaunt, a way he had never seen her look before. It was obvious to him that the worries of her father's illness had taken a toll on her. He was determined that she wouldn't have to weather this alone anymore. As for the shortage of funds for her father's on-going treatment, he had decided to help her out with that now, instead of having Shay worry about it because she wouldn't get a claim to the inheritance until the year was up.

He just had to convince her to let him help.

By the time he'd finished cleaning up the dishes, Shay had fallen asleep on the couch. He'd tried rousing her, but she seemed to be in such a deep sleep that he didn't try more than twice. Instead, he picked her up and carried her to her bed, but as soon as he laid her down, she stirred, groggily rubbing her eyes. He stepped away. "You fell asleep."

"What time is it?" she asked.

"About half past eight." It wasn't late at all. "You must be tired."

She sat up. "I'm not changed," she said, yawning, and starting to get out of bed. "But I'm so tired."

"Then just go to sleep," he told her, stepping towards the door to leave.

She slipped back between the covers and patted the bed. "Don't go just yet."

He cocked his head, not sure what she was asking him.

"I meant to stay awake so we could talk but your dinner was del—" She yawned a second time. "Delicious."

"I'm glad you liked it, now go to sleep, Shay. We can talk tomorrow."

"But I haven't seen you for days."

Something in her voice made him pay attention. "Sit here, just for a while," she pleaded.

How could he refuse her? He couldn't. He couldn't and he wouldn't refuse her a thing. So he walked towards her gingerly, and settled on the bed, on top of the duvet, almost at the foot of the bed, while she was propped up against the headboard.

"You never did tell me about the proposition your ex made to you that day." Her words threw him because he hadn't expected that they would be discussing Callie of all things.

"She wanted me to give her a job. She wanted to temporarily fill in for my employees that are going on maternity leave."

"She wanted to do the work of three women?" Shay asked, surprised.

He nodded. "She's not even qualified for the job, but she seems to think she can do it."

"She wants to be in your life, in any way she can."

"That's never going to happen." He'd see to it that it would never happen.

"She sounds determined," Shay replied.

She was probing, wanting to know if there was ever a chance for Callie to worm her way back into his life. For him, this event had as much chance of happening as a dog flying to Mars. "I can only handle having one woman in my life at a time." He waited for her reaction.

It was slow at first, the way her eyes darkened, and her lips twisted, as if she wasn't sure whether to smile or not, as if she wasn't sure what he meant. Maybe he was going to have to state what he meant in a way that left no room for doubt. "And while I've got you, I don't have eyes for anyone else."

"While you've got me…" she said, her voice lowering.

They stared at one another, and it seemed to him that they did this a lot, whether it was across the room, or across the table, or at a restaurant or on the hospital grounds. Only now that he was in her room, sitting on her bed and staring across at her, it was a whole new level of intimacy he wasn't sure of.

And he hadn't even kissed her yet.

Not properly.

"Do I need to worry about Ralph's niece?" she asked.

Her question made him roar with laughter. "Sometimes I feel tempted to tell him that you and I are together, just so that he can knock that crazy idea out of his head forever."

"What will we tell people? In the end, I mean? Assuming we can continue the lie."

"You really think that only Jenna will know that I'm living here? You told her I'd be here a week. What happens when she turns up on your doorstep in a month's time, and then a few months after that?"

She pushed her glasses up. "You're right. Something's got to give. You told my mom we're together, and now she won't leave me alone. She wants to know when you're coming over for dinner." She rolled her eyes.

"What do we do?" he asked, always wanting to take direction from her, doing what he felt was right for her.

"There is only one thing we can do," she replied. "We can play it by ear and see what happens."

He considered her suggestion. It was sound. It was the only thing they could do. And maybe things would unfold naturally now that the path ahead was clear for them.

"Lie down," she said, patting the pillow next to her. "Just for a while, so we can talk about Aunt Dena's will and figure out what we're going to do when the inheritance comes through."

"Lie down?" Was she being serious?

"I won't bite, I promise."

It wasn't her he was afraid of. She was too much of a temptation. He'd had a hard enough time trying to keep his thoughts to himself, and now she was asking him to lie down next to her.

"Don't you like thinking about the money and how it can

help?" she asked. "It's a game I have, and which I sometimes play, when things get too much."

She was thinking about her dad again, he guessed. "Okay," he said, forcing himself to overcome his hesitation. He could never refuse her, so he did as she asked, but made sure to lie on top of the duvet, so that they wouldn't touch.

And after a while, she lay down, too, and they both stared at the ceiling

"What will you do with the money?" she asked.

"I haven't thought that far ahead."

"I think of the money and all the debts I can clear."

His mood brightened. "I think of the new machinery and pay increases I can afford."

They laughed.

"Such big spenders," she pointed out. "But it's for the things that matter."

"No big fancy houses, or cars or vacations?"

"I might consider getting an apartment that didn't have a spider problem."

"You'll have a spider-free apartment for as long as I'm here."

"Promise?" she asked.

"Promise."

They started to make plans about how they would tell their close family and friends about the inheritance, and what they would tell them, and how they would have to take this secret with them to the grave.

He didn't know at which point it happened, but they fell asleep, because when he woke up the next morning, he was under the duvet, in bed with Shay, holding her in his arms.

❧

How childlike of her to expect that she would be able to navigate the tricky waters of living with a good man, a handsome man, a single man, too—and *not* fall in love with him?

She was in love with Blake, and had been for a while, but getting this man to see this was proving difficult. Impossible, even.

A week after she'd told him about her father's illness, after they'd fallen asleep in the same bed, things were back to normal. Blake had resorted to sleeping on the couch as usual, telling her that he didn't want them to rush into anything.

"But we're married," she'd cried.

"A lot of things have happened, Shay. Let's wait until your father's home, at least."

Wait?

For what?

He was a man of principle, but her body had discarded all notions of sense and sensibility, and she couldn't understand why he couldn't see the way she stared at him, or brushed her hands over his, or brushed her body as she walked past.

He seemed to have a willpower that all of her previous boyfriends hadn't possessed, but she was beginning to wonder if she needed to choke on something just so that he'd have to put his arms around her in an attempt to help her dislodge whatever got stuck in her throat.

She had considered seducing her own husband, in order to get him to kiss her, but so far she'd had no success.

Another week passed and despite Blake's snail's pace, everything else in her life was looking up. Her father had begun his third round of chemo, and it was going as well as that type of treatment could. She hadn't gone home this weekend, because her mom had asked her not to until this chemo cycle was complete.

She and Blake had left Kandinsky's with an ice-cream each

and had walked past the Knight Movie Theater where some new posters caught their attention.

"Hailey Ross's new film," said Shay.

"What is it? A romance?" Blake stood next to her as they stared at the poster.

"Action and adventure, it looks like." Helicopters and explosions were the background to an image of the actress wearing a leather jacket and shades and holding a grenade in her hand. "We'll have to come and see it."

"You mean, to the premiere?" Blake asked.

That was an idea. It would be another big event, lots of publicity, and cameras and press. And a lot of people they knew.

"Do you want to come to the premiere?" she asked him, finishing off her ice-cream.

"Do you?"

"We could go together," she suggested, in a déjà vu moment that reminded her of the night she they had spoken about attending the movie theater opening.

"Together?" he asked, his gray eyes all wide and twinkling.

"We could do things differently this time," she said, wiping her hands and starting to walk away towards the beach.

He followed behind her. "How differently?"

"I don't know. Maybe we could go together this time, and spend the evening together. Hold hands even."

"Like this," he asked, slipping his hand into hers, something he hadn't done since that time at the hospital when he'd turned up unexpectedly. They'd slept in the same bed a few nights later, and just when she had expected things to start moving, and changing for them, everything had come to a crashing halt.

"We could do that," she replied, sucking in a breath because the feel of his warm hand on hers did that to her. Blake taking her hand now made her feel funny all over again; made the small hairs along her arms suddenly soldier to attention, even though the sun was strong and she didn't feel cold.

"Do you think you could handle it?" she asked him, letting him rub his thumb along the back of her hand, while her insides started to bubble and churn.

"Oh, I can handle it," he replied, with a conviction that was hard to miss. "I wanted to make sure you could."

Oh, he did, did he? She turned to him, the sound of the ocean waves gentle and calming in the background. Grains of sand dusted her sandaled feet. "I can handle it," she returned, her eyes blazing. "I can handle anything you've got, Blake Kennedy, and probably more." She lay down her challenge.

"And more?" He stared at her lips.

Don't just stare, do something.

"Think we could spend all night together, like a couple, at the event, I mean?" he asked, and she wasn't sure if he was making a request or teasing her.

"It depends on what your definition of a couple is," she tossed back, enjoying the feel of his hands taking both of her hands. "Besides, we've spent all night in bed together, *sleeping.* " It was too late to disguise the longing in her voice.

"You sound disappointed."

She stared up at him, and decided that if he didn't make a move now, that she was going to kiss him. "Maybe I was."

Something flashed across his eyes, and before she had a chance to think about it, he dipped his head down and planted a kiss on her lips. His soft mouth on hers, and the electric sensation of his hands around her waist, pushed the breath clean out of her lungs.

"Still disappointed?" he asked, his eyes shimmering like water as he moved his head away.

She was still reeling from the after-effects of his chaste kiss when he slipped a finger under her chin. He lifted her face towards him before claiming her mouth and giving her a kiss that was warm, and mushy, and sweet. She melted against him as he kissed her deeply until they needed to breathe.

"Wow," she exclaimed, as they pulled apart, each eyeing the other with more than a look of hunger.

He lifted a finger and traced it around the outline of her wet lips. "I've wanted to do that for months," he told her.

Surprise slammed into her. "For months?" And all this time she had believed he hadn't seen her in a romantic way. He reeled her towards him and she willingly let him, enjoying the feel of his firm body. Yet this didn't seem like new, even though it was. It felt familiar, as if they'd shared this level of intimacy all along.

He cupped her face and gazed down at her as if she was precious. "Been in love with you for months, too." She felt suddenly dizzy, as if the world around her had tilted on its axel.

Blake loved her.

She savored the moment, letting his words sink into her heart and settle deep within. She stroked his face, her fingers sliding down to his shoulders, and then along his arms, over his muscles, feeling and squeezing. It drew a smile from his lips. "What are you doing?"

"I've wanted to do that for months." This man had no idea how many sleepless nights he had given her.

His hands squeezed her waist gently, making her heart beat faster because they were standing so close.

"Kiss me again," she urged him. He willingly obliged, and in so doing, set off a series of chain reactions inside her which were difficult to contain. The more they kissed, the more aware she became of his hands and body pressed against her. "Let's go home," she suggested. A walk on the beach was romantic and sweet, but she'd had enough of that. It was the passion and the sizzle she wanted. Seeing Blake's hooded eyes, it was plain to see that he felt the same.

Before they got home, they'd already made out in the car for the longest time, enjoying one another as if each kiss was their first.

By the time they burst through the door to her apartment, their arms were around one another, their mouths joined as if they weren't ready to part anytime soon.

Now that they were in a private place, away from prying eyes and ears, she wanted more. But Blake stepped away from her, just like she sensed he would.

"We did it all back to front," she said, feeling hot and sweaty all of a sudden.

"Uh-huh." He had his hands on his hips, as if he was assessing a difficult situation.

"We're already married, Blake." In case he needed reminding.

"Uh-huh."

"And I'm in love with you. I think I have been from the moment you caught that spider for me."

Something flashed across those cool gray eyes. A moment of understanding, enlightenment, perhaps, because his lips slowly curved into a smile. "Was that all it took?" he asked, his voice turning raspy.

"There were other things, as well," she answered, her face lighting up as he took a step towards her. "I've fallen in love with you every step of the way." Her heart felt squishy and soft, much like her insides.

"That's twice in one moment you've used the 'L' word," he noted. This time he took a step towards her. "What things?"

"I'll tell you later."

"Later when?" he asked, slipping her hands around her.

"Later, later," she replied, lifting up on her tip-toes and kissing him. It seemed to her that he'd been waiting for her words. Such a gentleman. It made her love him even more. He dropped another claiming kiss on her lips, the kind of kiss that would lead to more, and in the next moment he surprised her further; he slid his hands lower down and lifted her easily.

A rush of adrenalin surged through her body. He always surprised her; it was one of the things she loved about him. She giggled as she threw her arms around his neck and they kissed again.

"You mean *after?*" he asked, walking towards the bedroom.

"Yes, after." She left a trail of kisses along his face, as he walked into her bedroom, then closed the door behind them.

EPILOGUE

FOUR MONTHS LATER ...

*S*he was lying on the couch, reading a magazine when her phone rang.

"It's Frank Barclay, Miss Donovan." She sat up with a jolt, causing the latest edition of the luxury travel magazine she had been flicking through, to fall to the floor.

"Oh... well... hi there, Mr. Barclay. This is a surprise." She stared at Blake, her eyes and mouth making a big round 'O'. "It's Mrs. Kennedy, by the way," she reminded him.

"Of course," the lawyer replied.

"Was that a test?"

"I'm not at liberty to say."

She chuckled, then composed herself because it didn't seem to her that he was joking.

"How can I help you, Mr. Barclay?"

Blake stopped ironing his shirt, and picked the magazine up off the floor.

"This is just a routine call, nothing more, Mrs. Kennedy."

Routine call? This was the first time he'd called her since she and Blake had gotten married. "I haven't heard from you since we last met." She was curious. "How are we doing?"

"Very well. I see that you both like to frequent Fellini's restaurant."

Her mouth fell open. So, the spot checks had been taking place. "If you're ever in Starling Bay again, I highly recommend it."

"Thank you. I appreciate the recommendation. I understand you and your husband also like the ice-cream parlor?"

She stared at Blake. "Has that been a sighting too?"

"We've had quite a few sightings." He reeled off a few places that she and Blake had been to. Each sighting he mentioned was like a walk down Memory Lane, only, these sightings were real now. There was nothing false about them.

"You seem like a couple very much in love. I hope you understand that we needed to check, as per the stipulations of your aunt's will. You would be amazed at the lengths some people go to in order to claim inheritances."

She forced a tiny laugh. Blake set the iron down and came and sat beside her. "What's wrong?" he mouthed, but she shook her head. "Mrs. Kennedy?"

"Yes, sorry. You've caught me completely by surprise. I can imagine the lengths some people go to, but my husband and I are happily, blissfully married, I assure you." She stared at Blake, her insides filling with love. "Was there a reason for your call, Mr. Barclay?"

"No reason. You're approaching the half year mark next month. Time flies, and you will soon be in a position to inherit a large sum of money. You might like to give some consideration as to how this might impact your lives."

She swallowed.

As the months had passed by, she had been thinking about the inheritance more and more, and now that Christmas was upon them, and she and Blake were living their lives as a married couple, there didn't seem to be a point to hiding their love for one another from their friends and family.

They had been talking about revealing their secret.

But there was something else she needed to tell Blake. She needed to tell him that the sum they stood to inherit was so much more, so much impossible-to-believe more, than the half a million dollars she had initially told him. "It has been on my mind," she confessed.

"No doubt we will meet again in due course, Mrs. Kennedy. Merry Christmas."

"Merry Christmas." She held the receiver in her hands until she heard the dial tone. Frank Barclay had hung up.

"Hmmm. That was weird," she said, setting down her phone.

"It sounded weird." Blake lifted her legs onto his lap and massaged her calves. Ordinarily, this would have felt good. In fact it would have felt *great*, and she would have oooh'd and aaah'd appropriately. They'd have ended up making out on the couch, and then moved into the bedroom.

They had decided to move into Blake's house after Christmas. It was much bigger, and would be perfect for them. Because of that move, the need to let people know of their marriage would become more pressing.

But she had something else she needed Blake to know.

Something which had kept her awake at night.

A secret she no longer wanted to keep to herself.

They were attending their friends' wedding tomorrow, a few days before Christmas, and with so much going on, it had been difficult to find the right time. She had decided to tell Blake in the new year, not wanting to start the year holding anything back, but talking to Frank Barclay just now had pushed that all aside.

She needed to tell Blake now. She loved this man with every piece of her heart and soul, and the way he took care of her, the way he looked at her and listened to her, everything he did for her, and everything he was to her, told her that he felt the same.

"What's been on your mind?" Blake asked. "I heard you say that to the lawyer."

She sat up slowly, moved her legs off his thighs, set her feet on the floor, and leaned forward, twisting her body towards him.

His cool, calm eyes stared back at her in amusement. "What is it now?"

"That was the lawyer."

"I know. I heard. What did he want?"

She swallowed. "He was checking in. Making a courtesy call. He told me of the times they'd seen us, you know, those spot checks I mentioned?"

Blake's eyes narrowed.

"Fellini's, and Kandinsky's and kissing in the car."

Blake's smile was mischievous. "He sounds like a peeping tom. We need to pull the blinds down all the way when we're..."

She placed her hands on his forearm, needing his arm to hold on to, needing his support. "You remember I told you that you get half a million dollars at the end of the year?"

"Yes."

She swallowed, not sure of how to break it to him.

"Shay… tell me," he said slowly, his face filling with concern. He leaned forward, and cupped her chin. "What is it?"

"It's... it's not half a million dollars..."

He looked puzzled for a fleeting moment, and then, "I don't care about the money. If there's been a mistake, I don't care. It was never always just about the money for me, Shay. I only wanted to help you."

"You recall I said we had to be married for a year and then we could go our separate ways?"

His face turned somber. "And?" He looked worried.

"Well..." She took a deep breath.

"I'm not faking it anymore, Shay. This, you and me, together, this is real, at least for me it is." He stared at her as if she might say something that would break him.

She touched his face. "I stopped faking it a while back, too." Their love had blossomed from a seed of friendship, and it continued to grow every day.

"Then what's the problem?"

"I never told you what I stood to inherit, when you got the half a million. Did you never think to ask?"

He shrugged. "I wondered, at first, but it wasn't important."

"I stood to inherit a million dollars if we divorced after a year, and I decided to split it between us, so that we both ended up with the same amount."

He looked surprised. "You split it down the middle?"

She nodded.

"Any other person would have split it eighty twenty, with eighty going to you," he pointed out, "or seventy thirty, but you went for an even split."

"I wanted to be fair."

"You're fair, and honest, and generous, and I'm the luckiest man alive. Is that it? Because I need to finish ironing that shirt," he said, eyeing the ironing board. He started to get up. "And then we need to get ready for the pre-wedding dinner." He dropped a kiss on her lips.

The pre-wedding dinner was the last thing on her mind. "You never asked me what I stood to inherit if we didn't get divorced."

He slowly turned his head towards her. "Is that what you want, Shay? I don't understand why you're talking about divorce all of a sudden. I'm in love with you, and I don't ever want to get divorced." Fear flickered across his face as she shook her head. He put a finger against her lips, as if to silence her. "You're going to tell me something bad, aren't you? Is it more lies? I thought we were done with lying." He put his hand up when she opened her mouth to say something. "Just know that I love you more with every passing hour."

He looked sad, as if she had broken his heart into two. "I'm not talking about getting divorced, Blake. Sit down." She patted the cushion on the couch. "You need to be sitting down for this."

Something in her voice, or her command, made him pay attention and he did as he was told.

"My Great Aunt Dena left me…" She lowered her head, dazed. Even now, months later, she still couldn't get her head around it. And especially because, with the way things were now between her and Blake, it looked as if she stood to inherit the larger amount. "Twenty-one million dollars," she said, lifting her head and staring directly at him.

His mouth fell open, and when he didn't blink for a few seconds, possibly even a minute, she waved her hands in front of his face, trying to elicit a reaction.

"How much?" he asked, finally finding his voice.

She repeated the sum.

"Twenty. One. Million?"

"Yes."

"You can't be serious… you can't… no. This is a joke…"

She nodded her head, and kept nodding each time he said something. She understood exactly what he was going through, because she herself had gone through it before, only, back in the summer she had dismissed the notion of ever qualifying for the larger sum. She had been happy just to get the one million.

But these past few months with Blake had given her an inkling that she was on track to inherit the full amount.

"Twenty-one million," she said, in case he needed reminding.

He lay back on the couch for a moment, before getting up and pacing around the room.

"Twenty..."

"Twenty-one million," she repeated, almost getting bored.

"Are you sure this isn't a scam?"

"You've seen the documents."

"But the lawyer. He could be a scam artist."

"I've met him. He's real. This is real."

"Shay..." Blake swiped a hand at the back of his neck. "I don't even know what you would do with so much money."

"Let's not think about that yet," she said, standing up and in his way.

"Money changes people. I don't want you to change, I don't want what we have to be any different. *This* is my idea of heaven." He waved his hand around the room before locking his arms around her. "Isn't this what you want?"

It was the first time she had ever seen him look so apprehensive. "This is my idea of heaven. But since we aren't divorcing, we are going to inherit that money, and it will change our lives."

They stood with their arms around one another, forming an oasis of calm happiness even though this news had hit like a tsunami. "If we love each other, we'll find a way through this," she told him, for his shock was bigger, being so raw and so new.

"It sounds like a problem." He chuckled.

"Who would have thought inheriting millions would be so stressful, and what will we tell our family and friends?"

"We don't have to think about that now," he told her.

"We have a pre-wedding dinner to attend," she reminded him. "I would like to have a nice wedding," she said out loud, as the idea came to her. Everything about the Las Vegas wedding had been fake. She wanted the real thing, in front of loved ones, in a beautiful dress, and everything else.

"We can have an awesome wedding," he said, his hands sliding lower and resting on her hips.

She put her arms around his neck. "With a pretty wedding cake, decorated with little flowers and doves?"

"Anything you want."

"I feel better for telling you," she confessed. A huge load had been lifted from her.

"I don't know if I'll be able to sleep," he told her.

"You won't," she said, with authority. Not for another few weeks, for it would take that long to get used to the idea of that much money.

"Thanks," he groaned into her neck.

She squealed as he left tiny kisses along it.

"I want to tell my mom and dad," she said suddenly. Her father had had his fourth chemo cycle a month ago, and was recovering well. Blake had helped pay for all the tests, and ensured that her father was being seen by the best of the best.

Apart from the news that her father was on the road to recovery, she could think of no nicer Christmas present for her parents than to tell them the truth about her and Blake.

Though she had an inkling that her mother wouldn't be too pleased, and would feel cheated out of a wedding. But Shay would find a way to appease her. And what better way than to suggest they have a proper wedding in the summer?

By then, she hoped, with Blake's help, to find a way of telling her parents about the inheritance.

"You want to tell your parents that we're married?"

She nodded.

"And what about the inheritance?"

She grimaced. "That can wait."

He looked relieved for a second before asking, "You'll be wanting to tell Jenna, and everyone else, I expect?"

"We could mention that we got married in secret, but we don't have to tell them about the reason," she suggested. "We could say that we realized after being together for only a short while, that we loved each other, and we married in secret because we feared that others would think we'd rushed things."

"That's almost true."

She smiled at him, because it was.

Her Great Aunt Dena had changed her life forever and in ways she would never know. Through serendipitous circumstances, Shay had finally found the man who had been under her nose all along. A man she had never really noticed.

It would be difficult, almost impossible, to tell everyone the story of how they got together, of how this man was a friend before he became her husband, and a husband before he became her lover.

But none of that mattered anymore.

What did matter was that this was real.

No more faking, because this was forever.

Thank you for reading *From Faking To Forever*!

I hope you enjoyed Blake and Shay's story.

Winter's Vow is the next book in the Starling Bay series. This is the story of Dylan and Merry's wedding and you can read an excerpt at the end of this book.

If you'd like to be notified of new book releases and more, please subscribe to my newsletter here:

. . .

http://www.siennacarr.com/newsletter

Thank you,

Sienna

AN EXCERPT FROM WINTER'S VOW

CHAPTER 1

*L*ake Ivanhoe was cold in October. This morning the chill in the air near the lake was sharp enough to warrant a thick jacket, gloves and a scarf. Dylan wore his leather bomber jacket more these days because Merry loved him in it. She told him after they had started dating that it was one of the many things that had made her look at him in that way.

"Don't let Spart get in the water, Chloe!" Merry shouted, as her daughter ran on ahead with the great big beast galloping in front of her.

"Spart, NO! Spart....NOOOOOOOOOOO!" Chloe's cries echoed across the woods. Dylan got worried. Not about Spart's swimming ability, but because the lake at this time of the year would be so cold.

"Does he even listen to her?" he asked, as he and Merry walked hand in hand towards the lake.

"He listens."

Dylan wasn't so sure, sometimes it seemed to him that the great big mutt ran wild and did as he pleased. He craned his neck and peered in the distance, but, sure enough, Spartacus stood at the lake's edge, not going in any further. "He's listening."

"I told you. He'll never disobey her."

"She loves him," he observed. The way Chloe doted on Spartacus, and the way the huge beast followed her around all day, was endearing.

They strode towards Chloe and the dog. "She needs a playmate," murmured Merry.

"A playmate?"

She winced. She always did that when it was something she wasn't sure about saying. Only, she could say anything to him. Their relationship had developed within the year, and it wasn't until Meredith Nicholls had crashed into his life that he had realized what had been missing from it all those years.

He waited for her to say something, but she was uncharacteristically quiet. It surprised him, that she was being hesitant now, because they never held anything back from one another.

"A playmate, Merry? She has lots of friends at school. I'd say she's settled in really well, wouldn't you?"

"If she had a sibling. I mean, I know the age gap would be too much." She bit her lip.

They had talked about this before. About children, about extending their family. He considered Merry and Chloe as his family, even though he hadn't yet done anything about making it official.

But he had been thinking about it for months. He'd even bought the ring back in the summer, when they had gone out of town. She'd seen it in a shop, when they'd been casually looking at various displays of jewelry. He'd had caught her looking at the selection of rings, and he'd bought it on his next visit, because he had a desire to make their relationship permanent. He wanted to marry her. Didn't see what they were waiting for, except that he was hoping to get past the next few months.

Merry hated Christmas because her husband had died a few

weeks before. Proposing now didn't seem right. Maybe he should have done it back in the summer, but then he worried that it might have been too soon.

Not for him, but for Merry. Though she was strong and confident from the outside, he had come to know that she was soft and had her vulnerable moments. His role was to protect her, and he took it upon himself to always do the right thing by her.

It was better to bide his time, and maybe make a move in the new year. It had been difficult to keep his thoughts to himself because this wasn't the first time Merry had hinted about wanting to have a child. She had mentioned it a couple of times in passing, had planted a seed in his head. He hadn't really thought about these things much before. His love life before Merry had been up and down. He'd had his heart broken, and had concentrated on making his gift store into a success. His non-interest in romance had often annoyed his friends Reed and Rourke, but he hadn't wanted to go down the route of dating, not until he was ready.

And then he'd met Merry; she wasn't only his soulmate, but she had made him see what his life could be like—full, and happy, and joyous, with much more in it than just running his gift store. He hadn't met her, as much as she had collided into him, and while it hadn't been the most fortuitous of introductions, things had worked out wonderfully well.

They were meant to be together.

She was the one.

He saw himself growing old with her. Could see them having not just one child, but two, maybe three if that was what she wanted. Being with Merry, he found himself planning for the future in a way he had never done before.

"The age gap?" he asked, lost in his own thoughts, before catching her looking at him in an odd way.

"Thirteen years," Merry commented. "Maybe more."

He squeezed her hand, not understanding. "You've got plenty of time."

"It's not me I'm worried about. Chloe is thirteen. That's a huge age gap."

He had no siblings, but even he could see that that it would be a huge difference.

She was obviously worried, and it preyed on her mind. He could fix it easily, and he just had to set the wheels in motion. It was only a matter of finding the perfect time; sometime in the new year.

"All in good time, huh?" It was the only thing he could think to say, and he hoped it would be enough.

Her new life was so different. Less hectic, more joyous, with a future she was excited about. She wasn't merely surviving, the way she had been in Boston, she was living.

This was romantic, walking in the woods around her new home in Forest Heights, holding hands with Dylan as Chloe and Spart ran on ahead.

It was becoming a regular thing now, a long walk for all of them, for a few hours on the weekends, followed by lunch at her place.

How much her life had changed from a year ago. She didn't miss Boyd & Meyer, or the long working days when she would come home late with hardly any time to spend with her daughter.

These days, she worked as a freelance marketing consultant for a smaller department store out of town. Her week was split in a way that worked just fine for her: Monday through to Wednesday at the department store, and then on Thursdays and Fridays she would help Dylan with his store.

He told her that she was his lucky mascot, and that things had turned around for him ever since he had met her. She hadn't done much, aside from convince him to start an online store, so that he could sell his goods online and reach more customers. His store wouldn't have flourished were it not for the products he made. It was the gorgeous, handmade pet feeding bowls, and coffee cups, plates and vases, among other things, that people adored and bought as gifts that made customers come back for further visits, and spread the word by telling others.

She had also taken over the marketing and advertising side of his business so that he could concentrate on making and sourcing his products. As a result, the online store was becoming busier, and she and Laura, Dylan's assistant, shipped the orders and took care of customer inquiries.

This was why his store was now doing better than ever.

The only other change she had convinced him to make was to change the name from the bland Clearwater Gift Store to Fraser's. It was short, and memorable, and friendly sounding.

But this completeness to her life that Dylan brought, the togetherness, the loneliness his presence had erased, had also brought yearning for something else. She wanted to have another child.

A sister or brother for Chloe.

They had talked about it vaguely, and she sometimes threw it into the conversation at times when her desire consumed her. She didn't want to force Dylan into something he might not be ready for, but at the same time, Chloe was growing older, and was now a full-fledged teenager. This had ignited the fuse to the ticking time bomb of her own age. She wasn't too old to have a child, far from it, but as time passed, the age gap between Chloe and a new baby was lengthening. This was the only thing she worried about because things were perfect now. Her life was perfect. This past year had been about a new start for her, and for Chloe, and she liked to think she had made the right decision in leaving Boston and moving to Forest Heights, a place on the outskirts of Starling Bay.

Dylan lived not too far from her, about ten minutes in the opposite direction, and close to the store, but it wasn't ideal, them both living in different places. She longed for something more permanent. Roots, a foundation, a family home.

And yet she hadn't moved just to be closer to Dylan—even though she had fallen for him hard and fast. She had moved because she had fallen in love with this town. The way she felt about it now was so different compared to her initial reaction when she had arrived last Christmas, as part of her mother's carefully orchestrated plan with her friend Hyacinth Fitzsimmons.

Even if things between her and Dylan hadn't worked out, she had a feeling she still would have moved here. It was beautiful, peaceful and friendly.

When she discovered that Chloe loved it too, it made sense to give up her time-sucking career. Leaving the city, and her job there, had been the first step towards a more fulfilling life. The demands of being so high up in a management structure that rewarded hard work and great results had come at a cost. She had missed out on so many of Chloe's school events, but she could see now how she had buried herself in her work after the event that had changed her life forever. She should have been there for her daughter when she lost her husband, Chloe's father, so tragically, and so unexpectedly in a flying accident. But instead, she had kept herself busy at work, and let her parents take care of her daughter.

Now, a year later, she was settled and considered this her new home. Her romance with Dylan had grown and strengthened, and she felt as if she'd met the man who was perfect for her.

All that remained to make her life complete would be to have another child; a baby with Dylan. She glanced quickly at his handsome face. He was looking straight ahead, those now ice-blue eyes staring directly in the distance, keeping watch over Chloe and Spart.

He was tall, broad-shouldered, and good-looking, and when he wore that leather bomber jacket, something happened to her insides; they turned soft and mushy. Her heart would beat faster, just like it did when he put his arms around her and kissed her.

They saw each other every day, and ate dinner together in the evenings at her place, because she insisted on cooking, even when he offered to share the chore. She had missed many of those opportunities when Chloe had been growing up and now she wanted to be the type of mother who made everything, baked cookies, bread and cakes.

Dylan wanted everything to be equal, he wanted to do his share and seemed determined to not take her for granted, but she could see that he was busy with the gift store. He wanted it to be successful, and already he could see that she had helped turn a few things around.

She was content to let him focus on the business, while she focused on being the homemaker, a role she had given up before. But as was often the case these days, thoughts of a child seemed to cling to her.

While she sensed that Dylan had started thinking about the prospect of having a child, she didn't want to nag him about it. Naturally, it meant that they would have to get married first, and she felt like a shrew, herding him into a decision the more she spoke about it.

The only thing that annoyed her was that he seemed in no rush to make a decision to move things along.

She decided to let things lie for now. With Halloween, Thanksgiving and Christmas around the corner, the next few months would be extremely busy.

"What are you thinking about?" Dylan pressed his palm against hers as they walked, following Chloe and Spartacus.

"I was reminiscing about last year, and how I wasn't looking forward to coming here, and how much Chloe hated it once we got here."

"And look at both of you now."

"Things have changed," she agreed. "I've never seen Chloe looking happier."

"And you?" Dylan stopped and turned to face her.

"I'm happy too. I didn't expect to fall in love with this place, and I didn't expect to fall in love with *you*, but stranger things have happened."

He gave her a smile which reached deep inside her belly, spreading warmth to every part of her body. She loved his smile, and his dimple. The way he looked at her and made her feel whole and happy.

She was a lucky woman. A very lucky woman indeed.

But, what if he wanted to wait another year?

They hadn't really talked about getting married, only in vague terms, such as wanting to grow old together. Such as making some plans, about getting a bigger place together, eventually. He had only mentioned the 'M' word a handful of times.

Sometimes she felt needy, forcing the conversation to topics he had never had to think of before.

It's Christmas in a couple of months, she told herself. The season she wanted no part of would soon be upon her. She would wait until it was over with before talking to Dylan about their future.

Winter's Vow is available at all major retailers.

BOOKLIST

Whirlwind Kisses
Winter's Kiss
Maid for Him
Love Letters
Escape to Starling Bay (Books 1-3)
From Faking to Forever
Winter's Vow
Guarded Hearts
Table for Two
A Bouquet of Charm
Christmas Hope

For a complete list of books go to:
http://www.siennacarr.com/books

ACKNOWLEDGMENTS

I would like to thank my amazing group of proofreaders who check my manuscript for errors, typos and inconsistencies.

I am eternally grateful for their help and support. A special thanks to Dena and Nancy for their creative input with this story!

Marcia Chamberlain

Nancy Dormanski

April Lowe

Dena Pugh

Charlotte Rebelein

Carole Tunstall

I would also like to thank Tatiana Vila of Vila Design for creating the awesome cover.

Sienna Carr is the sweet romance pen name for an author who has been writing romance since 2013. She lives in the UK with her husband, three children, and a parrot.

Connect with Me

I love hearing from you – so please don't be shy!
You can email me at: sienna@siennacarr.com